HOME FOR THE HOLIDAYS

LOVING A PROJECT GIRL

TISHA ANDREWS

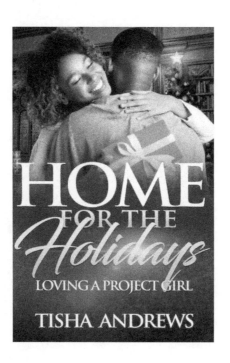

HOME
FOR THE
Holidays
LOVING A PROJECT GIRL

TISHA ANDREWS

Email: Authortandrews@gmail.com

Facebook: Author Tisha Andrews

Instagram: @lil_t_drew and @lil_tdrew

Twitter: @tisha_p12

Cover design: Michelle Davis

❀ Created with Vellum

SYNOPSIS

Ishmael Payne is all grown up, living the life away from home. On a full basketball scholarship to Duke University, top point guard in the nation, Ishmael is sought by many, yet what catches his eyes is not some college girl. It's a chick from the projects, snatching his heart.

Pepper Murphy, a local who never saw much outside the slum side of town, finds a job after graduation while most kids her age go off to school. She takes it in stride, carrying for he younger siblings and her deadbeat mother, Carrie.

When Ishmael and Pepper meet, an instant connection is made. When they do, he doesn't see a minimum wage liability—he sees a safe place to park his heart. Pepper goes along for the ride but something tells her there is more to Ishmael's life than letting her in.

He has a bitter ex and a petty mother, neither making it easy for him to move on or embrace what he wants most—that's Pepper.

Take a ride down south when Ishmael goes homes for the holidays, where things are not so merry nor are they bright. Yet, all is well because he has one thing he refuses to let go no matter how dim it looks for the holidays.

YEARS EARLIER

"Baby?" Chico whispered as he sat next to Myriah in the hospital. The beeping sound of the monitors was proof he'd almost lost her. He never feared much of anything in his life until he heard Myriah, his heartbeat, had tried to leave him.

Rushing out of the strip club, he told his best friend Keyz he had to go the hospital. Before he could ask why, he took off driving almost 100 miles per hour trying to get to her. His car, illegally parked in a handicapped spot, was almost left running. When he jumped out without turning it off, security yelled at him. He was so consumed with fear, he didn't care if his car was towed.

What mattered more now was Myriah and their son, Ishmael.

"Myriah, baby," he wailed, collapsing on her body until a nurse came in the room.

"Sir, please. She needs the rest," she whispered, placing her hand on his shoulder. "I don't want to have to ask you to leave."

Snatching away, Chico looked at her as if she was the enemy. It didn't matter he was the reason behind it all.

"Fuck that. I ain't doing shit. I'm staying right here until she gets up and comes home with me," he growled, wiping the tears that threatened to fall. He was a gangster, a beast but now feeling like failure.

"Please, sir. I'm trying to help," the nurse, staring back at the door. At any moment, security could come and take him away. That alone would only make matters worse.

"And where's my son? Why you in here monitoring me, but nobody can't tell me where my son is?" he snapped, heaving as his chest rose and fell. "Huh? Where is he?" That was the first thing he asked coming in and no one answered.

"Sir, he's safe with a neighbor. Look, she's fighting…fighting for her life. Can you calm down, please? I want you stay because she was asking for you. But if you don't, I will have to ask you to leave," she pled, motioning for him to relax with her hand.

"She really was asking for me? Chico?" he asked in disbelief, always hoping that she loved him as much he loved her.

"Yes," the nurse smiled, seeing his frustration subside just a little. "And I'm sure you want her out of here because in less than seven months, you two will be welcoming a little one into the world."

Full of emotion, Chico stared at Myriah in awe. All the dreams and talks they had of them being a family ran through his mind. There were days where he would get lost in her presence, dreading to go home to Meka his girl or worse when he rushed to get to her unnoticed by his crew.

He felt like this was a sign, a sign from God to live in their truth. For years, it was him and Meka until the day he met Myriah. She was loud, young and dumb but beautiful. Smart too, once he got to know her. She made him want to do anything, even more than selling dope.

However, he was big on loyalty. And since Meka was the reason he was at the top of his game, slanging more dope than he could pack, or count, Myriah remained his side bitch.

That and the fact she was also sleeping with his boy. To Keyz, Myriah was just "that girl", that hood chick from around the way he kicked it with and fucked off on for fun.

But to Chico, she was his heart. His whole heart.

Turning around to thank the nurse, he got the shock of his life.

There stood Keyz. He too got a call. It was from his son Ishmael, telling him his mother was in the hospital.

What he didn't know was the son he had loved for years wasn't his son and his best friend couldn't have been his best friend. He couldn't have. Not if he allowed him all these years to raise a child that was not his. He knew Myriah was an "ain't shit" girl, trapping him with a kid but he fell in love with that same trap called his son.

In that moment, Chico knew his friendship with Keyz was over. It had to be because there was no way he would let them all live in that lie. Myriah was his and so was his son.

It was time they confronted it all.

The lies.

The betrayal.

The broken bond.

But the one and only factor that kept them alive long enough to see another day was the same thing that broke Keyz's heart—Ishmael.

Years later, they both have to nurse the son they chose to love and raise together. Especially when betrayal comes lurking yet once again.

CHAPTER 1

"*Y*ou heard from Ish yet, baby?" Keyz asked his wife Iyana for the third time, walking in the kitchen. Ishmael was away at school, the youngest starting point guard in the NCAA at Duke University, dominating the game.

He passed on the offer to attend the University of Miami, itching to get away. He loved his family, but it was time to step out from underneath their shadow, gaining his own street credibility that started on the court. And from a relationship that turned sour.

In Miami, everyone fucked with him hard, knowing he was the offspring of the infamous Come Up Boys also known as The Crew. For years he struggled with wondering if he had a gang of friends because of that, often asked where his father was, no matter which one the person was referring to.

Yes, years later, Chico and Keyz decided to love Ishmael more than hate each other. And years later, he was the reason why The Crew, even after such betrayal, remained together. They learned how to put their differences aside, loving him hard and giving him the best.

He came to school with the best of clothes, rarely repeating outfits and when it was time to go on school trips, the kids never missed when he pulled up in a luxury vehicle like a Maserati or Benz, sometimes with security. Especially when there was not one but two king-pins that had a young prince they needed to protect.

Outside of material things, Ishmael Payne was pretty boy, too. A soft light pecan complexion, hair waved up like the ocean, with lazy, warm maple syrup colored eyes. His thick eyebrows, when furrowed, created a scowl that was deemed sexy by all the high school girls.

He had plenty of experience too, mostly right underneath his parents' nose and in their house. He had so many younger brothers and sisters, bad ones too, that he often could get away with doing the unthinkable as they tended to them instead, yet never getting caught.

Still, he was their pride and joy.

A nephew to his aunt Iyana, Ishmael almost forgot sometimes she wasn't his mother since he stayed with her and Keyz so much. With Iyana and Myriah being sisters, it was like one blended family.

That scandal could have torn them all a part but it's amazing what the power of love could do as they all couldn't wait for him to get home for the holidays.

"No, Keyz. He's young and hasn't seen his friends in what, almost four months? If I were him, I wouldn't be running home to see a bunch of old people either. I'm kinda surprised he's here with us," she told him, pulling out the ingredients to make Ishmael her infamous macaroni and cheese.

"Because we are the cool parents," Keyz said with a smile on his face. "And who's old? I'll show you what's old, woman," he told his wife, sliding up behind his wife as he felt all on her ass. Iyana giggled, lightly slapping his hand away.

She smelled like peaches, taste liked them too if you asked Keyz, always eager to have a taste of his wife inside of his mouth.

"The kids," she whispered, yet didn't move an inch as he slid his arm down around her waist and kissed her neck. "We can't."

"Yes the fuck we can," he told her, nibbling on her ear. "He better hurry up. We need a babysitter," he teased, popping her ass one time.

"Ugh," she fussed and laughed, pushing him away. "My baby is not coming home to watch *your babies*. You asked for them, you got them," she reminded him.

"Says the woman that can't stay off this di—

"Aye, I'm home!" they heard Ishmael yell from the living room, their eyes lighting up.

"Ishmael!" Cree screamed, running his way. She was their eight year old, the spitting image of her father. Ishmael lifted her up and kissed her all over her face, making her squeal. Two seconds later, KJ was right behind her, jumping up and down as he wanted for him to put Cree down. He was a big five year old, signs he was going to be tall just like his father.

"What's up, KJ? You getting stronger," he said, raking his hair as he hugged him.

"Miss me?" Ishmael asked his younger cousins.

"Yes," Cree sang, wrapping her arms around his legs. She wanted Ishmael all to herself since KJ had heir baby sister Kaison to play with. Cree hadn't warmed up to her yet, feeling like her parents betrayed her.

Kaison was too cute, with butter toffee skin and grey eyes like their mother. She looked like an African Princess, just one but a busy body tittering around the corner into the kitchen.

"Ma, can she go to daycare or something…forever?" Cree fussed, pinching KJ when no one was looking.

"Stop, ugly girl!" KJ growled, pinching her back. All the while Kaison raised both hands at Keyz, waiting for him to pick her up. His heart was full. He had all of his kids together again, as they all looked up to Ishmael.

Cree pouted, but even a pout couldn't dim her natural beauty. She was the perfect blend of her parents. Skin the color of coffee with dimples like her mother. Everything else was Keyz from her nose to full lips and long eyelashes. Keyz still couldn't believe he snagged their mother and neither could she. Especially since she was the dark skin church girl, the nerd.

"This girl," Keyz groaned under his breath, watching Cree hold on tightly to Ishmael. "Any other time, she's bad as hell. She sees you and now she's a bag of tears," he said, walking up to Ish. "Nigger you done got taller."

3

At 6'5", Ishmael was indeed taller than Keyz by one inch. Still he feared and respected him, never once going against his authority. Keyz would forever hold a place and position in his life like none other. Even his dad if her were being brutally, yet secretly honest.

"Daddy, tell Cree to gone now," KJ fussed, crossing his arms. "She's not the baby. Kaison is."

"No, you gone now," she shot back, looking around Ishmael as she stuck her tongue out.

Kaison giggled so hard like she understood everything going on. She was the roughest out of the Payne bunch, prone to be a tomboy. She'd fall and get back up, wrestle for hours and barely cried. Iyana always said God was tricking her by making Kaison so independent as she begged Keyz to wait a few more years before they had another one.

He wasn't sure if he could, enjoying how Kaison filled her mother's hips out even more. Naturally petite in size, Iyana still was. But three kids later, Keyz had more than a hand full of ass and breasts to hold. He could never get enough of her then or now, praying she'd give him at least another a boy.

"All y'all my babies," Ishmael declared, taking turns as he gave them each a kiss. When he did, KJ rushed into his arms about to knock him over.

"Whoa, KJ!" he laughed. "He got that speed and power, huh pops?"

"Cuz I'm big and strong," KJ growled then chuckled, flexing his imaginary muscle. Out of all of their children, he looked most like his mother. Their chocolate drop baby that had the warmest, grey eyes.

"Strong enough to help me and pops get my stuff out the truck?" he asked KJ who eagerly nodded his head 'yes'.

"Oh, you're staying with us?" Iyana asked, not wanting any tension with her sister.

"Yeah, why not?" Keyz answered for him. "This Ish's house just as much as it is any of the kids, baby."

"Yeah, auntie. Just for tonight. Don't trip," he told her, roughing up KJ as they play fought. "Who told you to grow this Mohawk?"

"Mommy said I could," he squealed as Ishmael tickled him. When picked him up and he put him down, KJ was ready again but this time he got in a wrestling stance.

"Whoa, don't hurt me," Ishmael teased him, watching the worried look on his aunt's face. "Look, they don't even know I'm in town yet," he admitted, hoping she would relax.

"Oh really? Why is that, Ishmael?"

"Baby? The food," Keyz told her, politely asking her to let it go for now.

He had no clue what was going on, but he knew Ishmael. He had his reasons for coming there first. The last thing he wanted to do was make him feel like he needed permission to be there. He knew Chico and Myriah might feel some type of way, but for now, he was being selfish. That was his fucking son, too.

CHAPTER 2

"*M*an, that sh—I mean the food was good, auntie," Ish said, catching himself.

"You know no matter how old you are or how big you get, I can and still will beat your butt, Ishmael. Don't play with me," Iyana warned him, hearing the other two kids chuckle. Kaison laughed too, clapping her hands.

"And what you laughing at, little girl?" Ishmael cooed, grabbing her leg underneath her high chair. Kaison threw her head back as he tickled her thigh, making her laugh even harder.

"Gosh, she so loud. Ugh," Cree mumbled, rolling her eyes. Secretly, she loved Kaison to no end, but it never failed when others came around, Kaison was the center of the show. Cree was another Myriah and Iyana didn't even know it. She had a mini men that acted just like her sister.

"Like you used to be," Keyz reminded her. "Still is," he said, stealing a kiss on Cree's cheek. He knew his kids well, their good and not so good side. Still, they were his babies. And there was nothing he wouldn't do for them.

Cree was a daddy's girl while KJ was a mama's boy. Now with Kaison, it didn't seem to matter as long as whoever was around fed her. However, he swore whenever he entered the room, he would hear "da da" first, waiting for Iyana to admit he'd won the battle of favorite parent. Kaison, however, never had a bad day, always balancing the energy of the house out.

"Which one of y'all watching a movie with me tonight?" Ishmael asked, baiting them after dinner was done. He had helped Iyana wash and dry the dishes, ready to relax.

"Meeee!" Cree yelled, raising and waving her hand.

"No, me!" KJ chimed in. "Me! Me!"

"Well, you can't if you don't straighten up those rooms, get a shower and into your pajamas," Iyana told them, reaching for Kaison.

"I can do that," Cree said, hoping up.

"Oh really?" Iyana said, struggling not to laugh. They fought her every time she mentioned the word "clean up" but not tonight. She silently mouthed "thank you" to Ishmael who watched her yawn a few times at the table.

"Ish, you're good" Keyz asked, wanting to know if he needed to talk. He was ready to slide up between his wife's legs, but he always made time for him if needed him.

"Yeah, I'm straight," he said, keeping it short.

"Alright now. You know how to find me," he told him as he stood up, kissing the top of his head.

"Pops, you do know I'm a grown man?"

"Not grown enough to take my money, though. All ten grand each month for real," he told him, speaking of his monthly allowance.

"Pops, come on now," he fussed and smiled, while Keyz kissed the top of his head once more. "The ladies can't know my you be kissing on me."

"The ladies?" Iyana said, walking back in on them. The last she heard, he and his girlfriend Mercedes were no more. It was sudden, but truthfully, she and Myriah were glad it was over.

Mercedes wasn't nothing but trouble to Myriah, but for Iyana, it was more about keeping the peace. She knew her sister well. Once she didn't like you, the world wasn't a peaceful place until she dealt with it.

"Daddy," Cree pouted, coming back quickly. "Can you let him go now? My room is all clean."

"Already?" Iyana asked, with one brow raised.

"Yes, ma'am," she sang sweetly.

"So I'm ma'am tonight. Hmph," she said, shaking her head. Cree was the sneaky child, but tonight she really was tired. So she would let her off easy for now.

"I'm done, too," KJ came in out of breath.

"Fine, but remember you can't watch anything that has what?" Keyz asked them, especially KJ who's mouth had a nice vocabulary of profane words compliments of sitting around his daddy and uncles when he shouldn't sometimes.

"Bad words," KJ said lowly, lowering his eyes.

"Right, and don't play. You know bad words when you hear them. Now, what about those baths? I heard that needed to be done too."

"Aww, daddy," Cree groaned as KJ took off, pouting.

"Bath, little girl," Iyana said, pointing to the hallway. "And hurry up. Ishmael don't run nothing around here," she said, giving him the eye.

"What, auntie?"

"Just take care of that cell that keeps ringing. And you already know my rule," she said, referring to girls coming in without her permission.

"I'm chilling with my family, auntie. Relax," he told her, kissing her on the cheek. "Pops, put your woman to bed. I'll be in the family room."

He laughed, hearing Iyana fuss at Keyz about letting him bring girls in all times of night. She could fuss all she wanted, his pops would make sure she was good and sleep if he did. But he wasn't looking for a female to chill with.

He needed peace, sort of stuck in a haze, trying to figure out his new situation. He had to admit Mercedes had him gone, but she fit the bill. She was eye candy and popular, the perfect arm trophy for the future NBA star he was destined to be. But his new girl was the absolute, yet had his head totally gone.

Once Iyana had retired for the night, Keyz decided to sit outside around the pool to smoke. He didn't do it as often as he used to, but he needed a moment to think. His son wasn't himself but before he ran him off, he decided to do his own investigation until he was ready to kick it with his old man.

He briefly scrolled through Ishmael's IG and Twitter, wondering what was his real reason for slipping in town quietly. At first, he didn't notice it until it hit him dead smack in the face.

A girl, but not any girl. From the looks of it, she was a baddie. A chocolate beauty just like his aunt, but rough around the edges just like his mother Myriah was coming up. She was the perfect blend, but definitely not what he expected. Especially not after Mercedes.

Without following her, he saw enough to know one thing and one thing that required a father and son talk right after the breakup he had.

"Shit, my son is in love," he whispered, gauging that love sick look on his face. "He's in fucking love. Damn, I really am getting old."

.

CHAPTER 3

THE DAY BEFORE CHRISTMAS EVE

"You have what I left you?" Ishmael asked Pepper as soon as she picked up. He was nowhere near sleep with Cree was sprawled across his lower legs while KJ's head was on his chest.

After watching *The Addams Family* and *The Lion King*, they both were knocked out. They were more than full after dinner, eating big bowls of popcorn Keyz made for them. He even snuck them some M&Ms just to steal a few hours away to be kiddie free so he could be with his Misses.

Kaison had one bottle before bedtime and was good and full, lightly snoring in her room she had alone. Cree refused to share a bedroom and since they had six of them, Iyana went all out giving Kaison her own.

"I told you I didn't want that, Ishmael," she mumbled. "I'm fine. You're only going to be gone a few days."

She loved the way he loved on her and was so protective, but now he was going overboard, making her strapped up. She wasn't surprised he carried, coming from the life his family lived, but when he was with her, his soft side showed up.

He was gentle, loving, nurturing yet a savage when it came to her. More so on the court, too. He was called "The Iceman" because he was cold, mean and nasty. He gave no motherfucking passes. If you got in his way, he took a charge and gave one, too. The hoop was his bitch and the rim was his side chick. He dominated the court from one side to the other and when he was there, nothing and no one got in his way.

Even with his current height, Ishmael was a beast at nineteen and he was still growing. He ate enough for two men his size and would still go put in at least five to six hours of practice a day and the weight room. He'd get so lost in the time, he barely realized when everyone was gone as he worked hard perfecting his body and skill.

Pepper knew how much he loved Cree and KJ. It was just as much as he did her siblings. Ishmael was young and talented and instead of him focusing only on that, he was trying to make sure they were all good. She hated that, wondering why he just didn't move on. She felt she had nothing to offer but pussy if she was being honest, but he never made her feel that way. Anytime she spoke on that, she would piss him off.

She was his black beauty, his rising star, his heart he'd tell her when he thought she was sleep. They still were in a place where they fumbled around with where they were going, but one thing was for sure—he was all in. She just didn't hope he'd wake up one morning and snap out of it. She admittedly was used to taking care of herself, but now with him around, he somehow removed that need for her to do that, terrifying her.

"Pep, chill ma. You refuse to drive my Tesla and now you catching the Uber. I'on like that shit at all."

"Ish, I've been catching buses all of my life. I'm not too good to do that now or take an Uber. I told you already. I'm not with you for what you have. I'm hood, boy," she laughed, shaking her head. "There's not a street I go on I won't know somebody. So you relax, baby. That damn car costs more than someone's entire salary a year or two or three of them."

"I never said you did and who gives a damn how much it cost? I had it brought of there *for you*. So you enjoy motherfuckers hollering at then riding in the comfort of my car, Pepper? The fuck I look like allowing you do that? I keep telling you that making sure you're good is *my job*."

"And my job is making sure I'm good, too. Ish baby, I'm not handicap, neither am I your responsibility," she said lowly, feeling the knot of money in her pocket. It made her feel like she did once before, many years ago. Used, bought and sold, but saying that would cause an argument she wasn't up for having. Besides, it was cold and the gloves she wore barely kept her hands warm.

"See," he laughed, trying to keep his cool. "That's where you're wrong. You are my responsibility, Pep. I chose this. I chose you. Stop being so damn stubborn. You know I'll be real fucked up in the head if something happens to you. You and the boys. Shit, I almost didn't come."

"Well, I'm glad you did and I'm sorry," she said, walking back to the front of the mall. She'd worked later than she was supposed to, but she needed the money. No matter how much money he threw her way, she was keeping a tally. To prove she wasn't a gold digger or using him, she had plans on paying every cent back while saving up for her own spot.

She'd done it all to make a dollar from working at the local bakery, a funeral home cleaning up after services to more. She'd be damned if she let her newfound, college basketball boyfriend make her forget those days. She'd stay broke before she let allowed him or anyone else to break her.

Some called her stupid. Especially her best friend, Sashay. But one thing's for sure—Ishmael Payne could have any girl he wanted. Every time they stepped out around town, she got confirmation of that. Bitches didn't care if he was with a woman or not. He was The Iceman, top point guard in all the nation.

To keep the peace, he shielded her as must as he could, but eventually, the world would know his new love interest wasn't some prissy college girl. Well, unless his mother found out first. That was his nightmare.

Myriah was complicated to describe and her outlook on life was even more complicated. One would think she would cheer for the project girl, but no, not even. She wanted the best for her son and Pepper didn't fit that bill. Her or anyone, if he were being honest.

Still, Pepper was more than where she came from. She could be sitting in a college class right along with him or anyone else because she had the grades. She also just had a weak ass mother who refused to apply for the ACT and SAT waiver test, which was needed for college.

That was Carrie, her mother's way, of holding her back. She'd been like that most of Pepper's life. Carrie's boyfriend, Craig and savior by the way her mother acted, had been locked up for the past five years, leaving Pepper to pick up where he left off. He was an OG, one who sucked at hustling but every now and then, he'd hit it big, coming in the door with bags of shoes and clothes and money for groceries.

Now no one was bringing in anything regularly accept Pepper. She never once cried about it—a natural mover and a shaker who did what she had to do. Always did, making it through high school without her mother's help, so she would keep making it.

With two brothers at home, twelve and thirteen, she had to. Besides, there was no way she was leaving Drew and Blake behind and making Ishmael take on three mouths to feed seemed selfish. But she was a package deal. When she ate, they did. Hell, even when she didn't, they did. That was Pepper.

Rent, even though it was Section 8 and only a hundred dollars, was her rent too. Carrie didn't care if the voucher wasn't in Pepper's name. That rent better be paid.

Then there was Richie, her brothers' father. They looked just like him. Skin as light as buttermilk, thick golden hair, and a slightly wide nose. Pepper's father was dead, or that's what Carrie told her. Had to be, since she looked nothing like any of them, including her mother.

Riche claimed her, but Pepper still felt like the black sheep whether her skin was dark or not. She didn't necessarily have daddy issues, but no man that ever walked through her mother's door represented what she hoped to have. Now with Craig in jail, Richie came through usually the same time Carrie's SSI check came in. Then was gone until that same time the following month.

Collecting checks from the government and Pepper too, Carrie had no care in the world unless it was Craig and if you asked Pepper, she didn't care if neither him nor Richie came back. She wanted her mother to fall on hard times, forcing her to get up off her ass but hard times meant her brothers went without and she wasn't having it.

In love, Pepper handed over half of her check and with the other half, she kept food on the table since Carrie, most times, sold her food stamps too. She also tried to give her brothers a few dollars, trying to keep them out of the streets that were already calling them. She couldn't turn a blind eye when gang members tried to entice them, but she threatened their existence if they even tried to be in one.

It was war going on. One in the real world, the one they lived in. The other in Pepper's world, starting with her accepting Ishmael's love even though she didn't felt she deserved it.

"You sure you have that on you? I know how you are about taking it to work," Ishmael asked her, hearing the voices of a few guys walking by. He was talking about her .22, something small but still dangerous when used.

"Yes, Ishmael."

"Good girl."

"You're such a butthole," she said and laughed, rubbing her hands as the night air numbed them.

"I'll be that, my baby. Where are the boys?"

"Uh, at home."

"Home or at Carrie's?" he asked, still pressing hard on his proposal for them to move in. It was a college apartment, but Ishmael broke all the rules. They somewhat had moved in almost two months earlier short of a few night here and there.

"With Carrie and don't start."

"I'm not, Pep, but that's fucked up. They're straight?"

15

"If you mean food and money, yes Ishmael. Anything else?" she said and yawned, growing tired.

"Naw, you sound just as bad as these bad asses I got over here," he said, staring down at his KJ and Cree. "This lil nigga KJ getting heavy. He's five and long, just like how I was," he said as KJ's legs dangled when he picked him up.

Cree, who slept wild, had already rolled herself off his legs, hanging on the edge of the sofa. He quickly put KJ in the bed before heading back to grab Cree before she fell. Petite, she wasn't as heavy, but did have a head full of hair all in his face.

Pepper knew how much he loved Cree and KJ. It was just as much as he did her siblings. Ishmael was young and talented and instead of him focusing only on that, he was trying to make sure they were all good. She didn't want to be the girl to mess up his up and coming star image, wondering why he just didn't move on.

She had nothing to offer but pussy if you asked her, and as far as she was concerned, he could get that from anywhere. Ishmael got pissed off every time she spoke like that. He hated she didn't see what he saw.

She was his black beauty, his rising star, his heart he would tell her repeatedly. She did for everybody else but herself, so he refused not to look out for her.

"But you're good? It's been..." he said, looking at his cell to see how long it had been since he hopped on the road. "Too long, Pep," he laughed. "I'm fucked up in my head, baby."

"Don't be. It's been better since I've met you," she whispered, missing him terribly herself. It scared her, rocked her world how quickly they became attached to each other. When she did admit that, she almost took it back.

"Yeah?" was all he said, stripping her soul open, but like always, she landed safely when he said, "Good, that makes two of us."

She cleared her throat, eager to change the topic and the mood. She had him all to herself for the past few months. He deserved to see his family, with or without her, so she refused to be a brat.

"Had a good time tonight? Linked up with your family and your friends? Old girlfriends?"

"It was straight and don't fucking play with me. No friends and definitely no old girlfriends. Blooney and Kev don't even know I made it in yet, Pep. I was just trying to get here so I can check in on you it.

Can't say if I'm still feeling this whole arrangement with you just not following my lead, but keep that line open, baby, when I call. Just listen sometimes and stop fighting me, Miss Bad Ass. Muhfuckas knocking people across the head over dumb shit when Christmas is not even about gifts. The streets would bleed if something happened to you, my baby," he told her, meaning that.

He would never admit to getting his hand dirty. Never had to, but he had handled business or more than a few occasions he'd never speak about. Him, Blooney and Kevin. They weren't The Crew, but they weren't to be messed with either.

"Don't do that, please," she asked softly, not wanting to get him all riled up. Ishmael was passionate about everything in life. Everything from basketball to getting respect. Then there was her.

"Don't do what, Pep? Pretend you don't matter to me?"

"I know I do."

"Then act like it. Where that fucking Uber?" he growled.

"It's coming, Ishmael. Just keep talking to me," she said, watching the parking lot thin out as the mall was closed.

"I am. I got you."

"You got me?" she asked, grinning as her heart fluttered.

She was close to mentioning the blogs, one showing him with a "mystery girl". The comments had her blushing but there were a few that made her pause. Especially one from his mother. Then she made her own post, showing their house off their house for the holidays.

Myriah Ramos, his mother, was the elephant in the room. He kept them a part as much as he could, even if he never would admit it. She couldn't blame him, but watching Myriah engage the followers was...scary.

And Myriah was stunning, a smooth, mocha complexion beauty

who was very articulate and business savvy. She was plugging Ishmael hard, already lining him up for endorsements when he hadn't even finished college yet.

"Always, Pep."

"So your mom? I like her," she said. She couldn't help herself, clicking on the post again.

"What I said about the blogs, baby? Make believe shit."

"Your mother loving her son is make believe?"

"That's not what I meant and you know it. I told you about moms. Straight hood from back in the day. She's… interesting, but she loves and goes hard for me. That's all. Just trying to secure my future. I leave her be as long as she don't expect me to entertain people that hop on there. It's an illusion, Pepper. No more, no less."

It didn't look like an illusion to her, reading a comment from someone who definitely had some kind of history with. Her name was Teresita. She, like his mother, was beautiful. A Latina with curves that killed the body game—a Miami Kim Kardarshian if she were being truthful.

But the one that caught her eye was this one named Mercedes. She wasn't too sure where she fit into his life since he refused to speak on his past, but she was flawlessly amazing. She had a hood flare to her too, but definitely had money.

She huffed lowly, knowing she couldn't compete with that on her best day as she looked down at her distressed, skinny jeans she bought from her Sashay, who sold boosted clothes on the side.

"Pepper?" he said, noticing how quiet she was. He wished she focused on them, hating he really did leave her now. "My mother is a hood mogul. That's what she does. Most are her plugging the family businesses." And there were a lot to plug from restaurants, food trucks, hookah bars, cigar lounges, and a shipping company.

The Ramos family went from pushing dope to pushing everything from food to furniture. His father worked hard to changed any gamed he touched and Myriah was responsible for most of that. Still, they were hood no matter what Pepper saw.

"What if she doesn't like me?"

"Who's your man?" he asked, sitting up as he began to fume. "Don't start that bullshit, Pep."

"Ugh, fine," she said with a chuckle even though she didn't feel like laughing as she rolled her eyes. "I'm done."

"Good. It's me and you, baby girl. You're fucking with a brand. Deal with it, but the real me is who you're getting right now. I'm hood, Pep. I can handle myself from an interview to the court. So, I can handle my moms. She knows I'm my own man. Just go with the flow," he said, unconvincingly. He didn't believe that himself, he couldn't say Myriah was a petty bitch. Even if she really was a petty bitch.

"Besides, my talent is mine. God somehow gave me that the second a ball hit my hand. When it did, a nigger started creating magic," he said and smiled. He loved the high he got when he was on the court, but he loved the high Pepper gave him too. More than she could imagine.

"Here we go. The big, infamous Ishmael 'The Iceman' Payne," she laughed.

"I am big, huh?" he said, referencing his hardened member he held in his hand.

"And nasty."

"And yours...remember that. And tomorrow, dead it. Drive the Tesla, Pep," he demanded.

"I will. Besides, I got your paper to finish. Then log on and complete your science assignment. I hate that group. Them bitches," she complained, thinking of the two girls in the chat that threw themselves at him.

"That's right. Get daddy right," he laughed. Ishmael was smart, but Pepper was smarter. He didn't care really what anyone thought, but he knew the moment his mother got a true whiff of how he was moving, she would start acting up.

She did it with Teresita and she never embraced Mercedes. So he knew with Pepper, she would have a got damn field day.

"Don't I always?" she replied, since she was completed most of his assignments whenever they chilled.

"Yeah, baby. Yeah, you do." Pepper was the shit. Myriah had to like her. She had too, feeling frustrated.

"The Uber's here," she said.

"I'm staying on until you make it in safely," he demanded. They chatted about his day and hers, in between sharing how much they missed each other. It was crazy, but it felt so right. Too right. If he could be in her arms and in her bed now, he would, wishing he would say "fuck his mother" but he didn't. So now he had to improvise.

"Hey, how far away you are from home? I want to see you," he said, his voice laced with lust.

"Ish," she whined playfully, looking up at the Uber driver as if he could hear him.

"I'm saying, that pussy, baby. You got a nigger right last night. Had me out there about to freeze my balls off waiting for you to come out before I got on the road. But that shit was worth it," he said, easing his hand in his boxers as he thought about his girl.

"Yeah?" she said, her feelings all over the place.

They ordinarily would have been at his place, but she refused to stay there when he wasn't there. When compared to his, her place was small. So small, she slept in the living room on a pulled-out sofa. A Chinese divider she found at a thrift store offered her some privacy, but not much. The other two bedrooms were for her mother and brothers. The divider wasn't much, but it was enough if it meant her brothers slept good at night.

She already knew how Ishmael lived, social media giving her the deal with that too. She must have sat for hours, saying "wow" and "oh my" scanning every photo posted on IG and Twitter right after he first stepped to her.

It was that big money, driveways lined up with three to four luxury vehicles, pools, Jacuzzis, and gazebos out back were proof he was living a life she knew she never would. Two story houses with more bedrooms and bathrooms than five to six apartments in her building. He mentioned something about a marketing or PR team, Gush R Us, which blew her mind.

He wasn't lying. He was hood royalty while she was just hood. So, him chilling in on a six-inch mattress with General Dollar sheets still blew her mind. Especially hearing the girls around campus have his name coming out their mouths. She wasn't a fool and she wasn't up for being a charity case.

Her place, surprisingly, was clean as much as she stayed on her siblings. Yet she cringed each time Ishmael forced his way over there. She'd already tried twice breaking up with him, the last time ended up with him refusing to suit up for his game if she didn't open the door and let him in.

This first time he came over he was clear, telling her, *"I don't care about where you stay, Pepper. How you live either. That's your current situation, but not your permanent one. I told you, when I make it, we make it."*

And he'd been solid ever since. He grabbed his joint as he closed his eyes, thinking about her. He had a woody that would knock her insides loose, eager for her to step inside. When he heard the door opened and closed, she said, "I'm here in the building."

"Good. Keep walking before I have to hop on a jet, shorty. You know I hate that shit," he fumed, meaning it. He knew the streets were mad busy with fiends and dudes trapping on each corner.

He gave no fucks, coming over there packing. He was a hot head, too. She'd seen him in action already, getting a mild version if she knew his real history. When he first learned Keyz wasn't his father, his behavior was out of control.

He was fighting, skipping school, even seeking out attention as he linked up with a local up and coming gang. That didn't last long though once they learned his identity.

He was born a Payne, still carried the name but the Ramos blood ran through his veins. The streets feared both, Keyz and Chico, refusing to put him on, but the definitely respected him whenever he showed up.

A few kids lost a few teeth and one boy arm was broken. Ishmael was on a fast track to juvie but Keyz had an idea, forcing something in his hand—a basketball. It was Keyz's first love too, but poverty forced him to abandon it.

Ever since then, Ishmael had been a basketball sensation from middle school until now. That alternative led to many conversations with boosters, sneaker companies, and even Gatorade executives. He was lethal, so fucking lethal and he was all hers.

"Sup, Bone," she said, speaking to her ex, hoping he'd let her go by as she held the cell up to her ear. His aunt lived a few doors down where he chilled from time to time.

"Why you do that?" Ishmael snarled, gritting his teeth.

"Just did. He's cool, but you know how y'all are. Whenever other men are around, y'all feel the need to flex. Bone knows I'm not interested but no harm in speaking, Ish. Don't trip."

"Oh, okay. So, fuck what I say? Bet," he grunted. He trusted Pepper but little shit like that made him feel like she took that college, basketball rep he had as him being soft.

She was tough, independent and had a slick mouth. All three he loved about her. Her body too. It was sick. She had breasts, hips, and ass for days with a washboard stomach. Her hair stayed either plaited or box braids. It was cheap yet still trendy, something Sashay would do for her for twenty, or maybe thirty dollars. Still, no matter what how she wore her hair or the clothes she wore, he'd proudly say "that's me".

"I don't want to fuss. I don't," she grumbled, slowly sliding the key in the lock and unlocking the door.

It was after midnight. She exhaled when she stepped inside, the dim light from her cell guiding her to her corner where most of her clothes were neatly stacked up in bins.

"Yeah," he huffed, trying to get his mind right. Pepper kept him wanting to stay on her ass, but she had him wrapped around her finger. Even if he never wanted to admit it. "Just call me on that Facetime when you get in that bathroom, Pep."

"Okay, I'm on my way." She grabbed a fresh pair of panties, a pair of pajama bottoms, and a t-shirt. It was warm, the heater blowing but she would never sleep without clothes. Even if she didn't sleep in the living room.

Carrie was a poor judge of character period, possibly bringing anyone in there on her. So, she slept used to sleep with a knife under her pillow until Ishmael got her a gun.

By the time he heard her secure the bathroom door, he switched over and dialed her on Facetime, refusing to wait.

"Ugh," she groaned, hating how impatient he was. "I still haven't gotten undressed," she whined, sitting down on the toilet as she propped the cell up on the sink. The bathroom was small but clean, something Pepper did not play about.

"Well hurry up, baby. I need to go to sleep, but I need my fix first," he said lowly, watching her nipples pressed firmly against her uniform top. "Let daddy see his pussy, baby." He scooted down, now flat on his back, watching he as she undressed.

Pepper even gave him a little show, intentionally pulling her shirt over her head as she flexed her stomach muscles.

"Hurry up," he demanded, eager to see her breasts. She was wearing the bra and panty set he got for her a few weeks back. It was tangerine, which glowed against her chocolate skin.

When she lifted her arms up to pin her hair in a bun, he inhaled then exhaled, stroking his penis. His breathing was slightly labored as eased his hand up and down slow but hard, feeling the slickness from his pre-cum ooze out on his hand.

"Pep," he said in a quiet, hushed tone. "Hurry up, baby. Damn," he hissed as she stepped out of her laced underwear. "That pussy the fattest, babe. Sooo fucking pretty," he hissed, tasting her slickness in his mouth even now because she stayed on his face. Sex didn't happened that often, but when it did, "got damn" was all his brain come up with.

"Sit back and spread 'em."

At this point, Pepper was horny herself. Hearing his voice alone made her crave him just as much as he craved her if not more.

A fresh shave a few days earlier still revealed fattened lower lips, milk chocolate like a Twix bar that bloomed when she pulled them apart. Ishmael was in love—in fucking love, sitting up as his wood stuck up straight in the air.

Pepper saw it, hissing as she waited for him to tell her what he wanted to do. And whatever Ishmael asked for, he got it. She wasn't that experienced, but in no time, she was his pornstar. He was spoiled already period in life, but Pepper had spoiled him even more. She couldn't buy him nice things or treat him out on dates occasionally like some girls do, but what she could give him, she gave and he loved it to no end.

"Babe?" he said, his voice shaky as he roughly worked his dick, the sight of her pussy was making him shudder.

"Yes, Ish?"

"After I bust, I'm sending you a ticket. Call out for a week or shit, fuck that job. You're spending Christmas with me," he said, losing all his composure. He knew his mother would be acting up, but when it came to Pepper, common sense was straight nutso. He'd own that and by her house right about now to get her to come. "Touch that pussy, slide that finger in my shit. The one with my ring on it."

She did. "Now, another one," he coached her, watching he cream up nicely as they slid in and out. "Rub my fatty," he said, referring to her clitoris. It was indeed engorged, glistening as she threw her head back, enjoying the ride.

"What about... what about the kids?" she asked, biting her lip as she dropped her head down. Her gaze met his. It was intense, telling a story of two people. Two people in love that made their own rules.

"No worries. I got that. Now bust it for me, ma," he grunted, his spill spurting out prematurely. "Ahhhh fuck!"

Pepper sat up and stopped, covering her mouth. He fought hard to stop it, but it was too late, splashing on his cellphone screen.

"Baby, no," she said, a slight chuckle followed. "We just started."

"Hell yeah. Now hurry up and shower so I can bust again. Round two, Ima make my pussy skeet for me," he growled, slightly embarrassed.

He had plenty of vagina over the years, but none grabbed and tugged on his dick like Pepper's. Probably because she was rationing it out, but whatever it was, it was like the best crack in town.

She was just like her name—small, feisty yet hot as fuck. And he wanted her just the way she was. He wanted a girl that had nothing to offer, but had everything he needed at the same time.

"I love you, Ish...with everything in me," she said, feeling fragile. Her own voice was unfamiliar to her when she said it, but it felt right, scaring her even more but it was the truth. Ishmael Payne had her whole fucking heart.

"I love you more, Pepper. You're all me, baby. Just stay out your head," he said. "Stay here with me...forever."

CHAPTER 4

JANUARY 2019

"*B*aby, stop," Mercedes whined as Ishmael had her pent up against the seat of his 2019 Tesla. It was an early graduation gift from his parents. They tricked him, telling him the school wouldn't let him bring a vehicle over the summer, only to give him his dream car six months earlier.

He'd been pouting all week when he didn't get it for Christmas, driving his Range Rover like it was a beat up hooptie that everyone took turns driving in the hood. He didn't ask for much, but he'd been eyeing them online for months, finally getting one right after their annual New Year's family get together.

His mother couldn't take all the whining while Chico told her to let the boy live a little. He also didn't want Keyz and Iyana to beat him to the finish line, snatching his son up one first.

It was true he and Keyz learned to co-parent, but Chico would never lie and say he still didn't feel like his position wasn't threatened. He'd never take it out on Keyz since it was him and Myriah that fucked around behind everyone's back, but his children were all he really had in life to be proud of, starting with Ishmael.

So anytime he felt he was coming up short, even when he really wasn't, he did dumb shit like buy his son a Tesla. A customized, yellow one with chrome rims at that. It was sick, the first to hit the street of it's kind, but the smile on his son's face was worth it. That and the one on Mercedes face too, since he stayed trying to fuck her in it.

"Stop what?" he spoke in the crook of her neck, smothering her with kisses. She squealed, feeling his hands slowly work their way up her dress. They'd been with friends all afternoon at a local hang out spot, reminiscing about their senior year so far.

Homecoming was coming up and they both were running for homecoming king and queen. Mercedes, a top cheerleader, wasn't a shoo in to win, but Ishmael was. She was hated by all, but to her, it didn't matter. However, as long as Ishmael Payne kept her full of dick and on his arm, she'd take that L when it came to wearing any other title.

"That," she groaned as he massaged her breasts. "We have to go shopping for your tux and my dress," she moaned, feeling the moisture pool build up between her legs.

"And we will, Cedes. Tell him to calm his ass down," he whispered, pecking her softly a few times on the neck. He then placed her hand on his rather endowed manhood.

"I promise I will take care of him really good, baby. But if we don't get inside, your mother will kill us. She already hates me," she pouted, cupping him by his cheeks as she slipped her tongue in his mouth.

Her speech didn't quite lined up with her actions, but Ishmael wouldn't stop her. His mother knew what time it was, even though they were sitting outside in the driveway. He was no angel, never pretended to be but she'd been holding out all week long.

"Fuck," he groaned in her mouth as she cupped his dick. "That's your word?" he managed to ask, pulling and sucking on her bottom lip.

"Yes, baby," she hissed, kissing him once more.

She loved he couldn't get enough of her. Especially since she knew he wasn't one hundred percent faithful. She didn't get him fairly, so she knew Teresita, his ex, still came by from time to time.

They hated each other. Always did. But what Mercedes wanted, she had always got. Pretending to be the friend Teresita needed to cheat, Mercedes got just enough intel to send Teresita packing on her way. She'd been with Ishmael for a year, a mixed Spanish mommy. She came in knocking bitches to the back her freshman year while Ishmael was a sophomore. It took her a year to wear him down, but a year to lose him.

By the time Mercedes was done, it was Teresita that was playing the side chick, side bitch, and any other side that was a side. Ishmael denied it every chance he got, but Mercedes didn't care as long as her pockets stayed lined up nicely and she was on his arm publicly.

She learned one thing from her mother Paris early on. That's never step down off your throne to confront a bitch that was dethroned. Teresita was last year's pussy and if she had it her way, by the time he left for college, she'd be a real thing of the past.

Mercedes couldn't wait to step on a college campus with Ishmael, heavily sought by the top ten NCAA colleges. She was smart, and could have any man she wanted, but to be with Ishmael meant she solidified her future, ready to have a gang of his children whether he put a ring on it or not.

Her father, Big Wayne, was a well-known former gangster, now the owner of a chicken wing franchise amongst other things from car washes to laundromats. Mercedes was his only child, wearing diamonds before she could even sit up. So Ishmael would be the perfect transition to keep the diamonds coming in.

Her mother lucked up being the only one to trick Big Wayne, hiding her pregnancy until it was too late to have an abortion. He refused to even speak to Paris, telling her to call him when she went into the labor.

But the day he saw Mercedes, he knew she was his. Full lips and a fat, round face with slanted yes and long eyelashes. Her color wasn't in but around her ear was a tad bit darker, signs she would be close to his complexion since Paris was what they called "high yellow".

Paris did nothing but hustle men out of their money, working at the local bar where Big Wayne and his boys hung out every Thursday and Friday night. Saturdays were for his girl back then, Tootie, and Sundays were for his mother.

All it took was one night. Big Wayne had a little too much to drink and Paris came to his rescue, making sure he got in safely. When she tried to leave, she soon learned why they called him *Big Wayne*. And every chance she got, Big Wayne kept reminding.

After Mercedes was born, Tootie decided she wasn't competing with a baby. And being a stepmother meant she came second for at least eighteen years. That left Paris to graduate to the main spot who soon became a kept woman. Big Wayne never fell in love with her, but she was a great mother and solid, cutting any dude off once he decided to wife her.

She was smart too, eventually giving him the idea of how to clean his money. Even helping him run his businesses. By the time Mercedes was five, she recognized her family was filthy rich. She never wanted for a thing then and now, being Ish's girl.

A tap on his passenger window freaked Mercedes out as she screamed, "Oh shit!"

They both looked up to see his father Chico. He was grinning, remembering those days when he got lots of ass in the front and back seat of a car. On top of the hood, too. The difference he didn't do it on his parent's dime or in front of their house. He couldn't, not when he the streets raised him.

Stretching his eyes his son's way, Chico assessed what his son was in store for. Girls like Mercedes came around all the time, following the paper trail. To Chico, she could be trouble. Especially since Myriah wasn't feeling her. An expensive one if she was right. But instead of shitting on his son, he decided to just be there and ride it out with him, hoping he avoided a pitfall.

"Roll it down," he told his son, who sighed with his hand still up his girl's dress. One look made Ishmael quickly sit up, pulling Mercedes's dress down. There wasn't much dress too pull, too short for Chico's taste but enough to explain why his son was ready to tear her ass up.

Mercedes was that chick.

That girl.

That bitch that every dude on the block, around the block and close to the block wanted but couldn't have her. At least not without the right amount of commas in the bank, hoping his son wasn't being a trick for possible sneaky pussy.

"Mercedes?" he said, speaking with an edge to his voice.

"Hi, Mr. Ramos," she said and laughed nervously, sitting up as she tugged on her dress some more. She adjusted her top too, as he looked straight ahead at his son instead. "We were just about to come in," she lied, elbowing Ishmael in the side.

"Aye, your elbow hurt, crazy girl," he fussed, stretching his legs to hide his boner.

"Son, we have less than two weeks. Your mother has been preparing this dinner for months. I keep telling her this just a fucking homecoming event, but you know her. Everything has to be some big production and shit." He laughed when he caught himself rambling, noting Mercedes was sucking his wife's perceived weakness up.

Myriah had come a long way, proving she was more than a nut he caught many days. Besides, he loved her dearly, glad he'd caught himself before it was perceived he was disloyal to his wife. Those days were gone, shutting it down before Mercedes had something to run with later on that could be used against him.

She was a pretty little thing, observant too. He knew her parents very well, especially her father and respected him, too. But that didn't mean Big Wayne knew how his daughter moved. Chico didn't want to be the one to expose it if his gut was right, preferring she fucked up some other kid's life, truth be told.

"Anyway, when you fuck up, I got to hear about it. So wrap this up in here and get ready to spend time with your family," he firmly advised, then looked Mercedes' way. "That means he can't be all up under you, Miss Lady."

"Of course not," she said, batting those slanted brown eyes. Anytime she did, Ishmael would smile liked he'd seen her for the first time.

His parents didn't have anything against Ishmael falling in love.

Just not now and with two parents that took years to get it right in life., Chico wasn't so sure if his son knew a healthy love or not and if was more than likely his own fault. He and Myriah were a mess. He owned it. He just hoped his son wouldn't pay for it now as Mercedes subtly shimmied in her dress as she stood up.

"Son?" Chico said, leaning down to get his attention.

"Yeah, dad?"

"Let's go *now*." He tapped the hood of the car before he walked off. He hoped they were right behind him as he refused to look back.

"Maybe I should have gone with my parents?" Mercedes said with her lip slightly poked out.

"Girl, for what? I told you my mom sent then an invite to come here," he said, sliding out and closing his door. As he approached her, he motioned her over with his finger. "Come here," he growled lowly, gripping her chin. When he did, their lips were close. He gently pecked them and whispered, "Stop running from me, Cedes. Why the fuck would you not want to be here? Ain't this our time, king and queen?"

She loved whenever he called her that, dropping her eyes. She fought not to smile, but when she did, he knew he had her.

"Yeah, don't forget who runs this," he told her, lightly cuffing one ass cheek. He would fuck her outside if he could, wondering if he had enough time to do just that.

"No, they are already waiting. You know how your mother is. She already thinks I'm stealing her precious, baby boy," she said, not moving an inch as he relished in all that ass he had in his hand.

"True," he laughed. "Myriah's crazy as fuck."

"You said it, I didn't," she grinned, but wanted to tell him he was right. Her mother already put her up on Myriah's antics back in the day, wondering why she thought she had the right to speak on anyone. But she'd never say it, even if he was in love with her. Love didn't seal the deal, a baby seemed to, so she remained quiet.

"She is, but that's my ole lady right there. Love her ass, but look at me. Of course, she loves her baby boy," he said, backing up as he looked down at himself. "I'm a fucking masterpiece," he said, arrogantly.

He was Balmain down from head to toe, a Rolex watch on one wrist with one iced out chain that carried a skull head. When asked why he got it, he said, "Because I bury motherfuckers on the court."

"Now come on inside so we can get this over with," he told her, slipping one hand into hers. "And pull that dress down, too" as if there was more dress to pull.

No matter how much he pretended he didn't care what his mother thought, he really did. He had more condoms than three clinics and always got the "strapping up" speech right before he stepped out. Even when Mercedes was around, albeit in a polite way, followed by his mother's infamous smirk. Still, she had paid her dues and as long as Myriah didn't piss her mother Paris off, Mercedes wasn't going anywhere in his eyes.

As the approached the door, Ishmael had to get in one more feel as he gripped her ass and bit her neck.

"Ish, baby. Stop," she whined, yet gave him more access as he slid his tongue up her neck.

"You sure you want me to stop?" he asked, giving her a look.

"Only for now. You heard your daddy. It's time to celebrate, baby. We did it. We finally are nominated king and queen, about to leave this bitch in a few months, too. You off to Duke and me, well I'm still deciding," she said, still not revealing all of her plans.

"Bout that," he said. "You can always come and chill with me. I know you're worried about what everyone thinks, but fuck it. That's another motherfucker's opinion. Not ours."

When the door opened, she firmly pried his hand away from her ass, ending a conversation she wasn't ready to have at this moment. He real goal was to be a fashion designer, modeling her own clothes. She'd seen many young women doing it, never stepping foot in a college classroom.

She loved everything about fashion, but saying that made her look shallow. So she opted to buy herself more time until she could finalize her approach that was on *his* dime.

"Mrs. Ramos," she greeted and smiled. "We were just coming in. Right, Ishmael?"

"And I was just coming to make sure you two were. Hurry up now. Everyone is inside but you two and we are ready to eat. Your parents coming?" she asked Mercedes, never hearing back from them.

"Uh, I think so. Let me check," she said and lied. She hoped they didn't since Paris despised Myriah. Anytime she saw her on a blog or down her social media timeline, she gagged.

As she did, Ishmael whispered, "Baby, the boys out back. Come on out there when y'all done doing girly stuff." He laughed when he did, hoping she played nice.

Myriah wore a little scowl, displeased with the hold Mercedes seemed to have on her son. She owned her former promiscuous days, thus her reason for not trusting Mercedes and her scandalous mother at all.

She knew Paris very well from when they were younger. She was a few years older, often seen in the latest D boy's car back in the day. She was a natural beauty, heads turning even from the girls. Her own parents were known back in the day for selling dope, landing them in federal prison.

Paris was left out there, just barely eighteen, but she made it work. What she didn't earn working at the bar, she earned it by the men she kept. She wasn't a known whore, but if she was seen with anyone, he was definitely lining her pockets with money. To her, Mercedes was just like her, just more discreet, disguising her true intentions.

"They're coming," she said, hoping they would forget the lie she told later on when they really didn't show up.

"Well, perfect. Until then, you can place your purse in the guest room and follow me in the kitchen. That's where all the ladies are. Last minute things," Myriah said and smile, lifting both brows as her eyes rested on her dress.

"Of course," she said. She sighed, rolling her eyes when she gave Myriah her back. "Her old whorish ass," she mumbled, placing her two thousand dollar Louis Vuitton bag in the closet. She didn't want to, not knowing who all would be in there. She wished his family

34

learned to leave some stuff in the projects, but a few of his cousins and other relatives clearly were very much enmeshed in that life.

Mercedes wanted no parts of that crowd and admittedly, in front of her father, her mother didn't either. Big Wayne, however, was different, but that's why everyone loved him. He had money, but still remained level-headed.

He spoke highly of Ishmael's parents, shutting Paris down anytime she did try to speak negatively about Mercedes' potential in-laws. But in her eyes, her mother was right. They were borderline low class and his mother was nothing but a cleaned up whore.

She loved Ishmael, she truly did. But she knew if his mother had her way, she'd try to turn Ishmael against her, or he would never leave some of this hood lifestyle behind him.

"You're done?" Myriah asked, sticking her head back in the room.

"I am. Had to use the restroom," she lied again, something that was becoming easier to do, as she pulled that dress down yet again.

"Too late for that," she mumbled as Mercedes walked passed her. She heard her, but chose to ignore her. She only had to impress one person—her man. It was clear she did, when he stood at the patio door staring her down with lust in his eyes.

"Gone on now," Myriah instructed her. "Ish, go check on your sister and brother by that pool. Be productive besides gawking at her," she told him, smirking.

"Ma, I—"

"Ish?" he father warned him, walking up behind his wife.

"Okay, dad. Sorry, ma. I love you." He shot her the perfect smile, looking so handsome as he warmed her heart.

"Love you more, baby. I won't hurt her."

"No, but my behind will!" Rickey said with a snap of his finger. "Honey, this dress. Yasss," he sang with two snaps, motioning for Mercedes to twirl around.

Myriah pushed Mercedes along, rolling her eyes at him. She loved Rickey to death, but he picked the wrong time to play. They all knew how she felt about Mercedes.

Mercedes snickered, then winked her at Rickey. If she got a transgender man to look her way, the dress did exactly what she wanted it to do. And there was nothing Myriah could do about it.

While the women attempted to put Mercedes to work, finishing up the banana pudding, Ishmael sat outside around the pool with all the men charged with supervising all the kids. He was glad he could kick back and relax, quieting all the noise down about him and Mercedes. He used to be a hoe himself, many still in disbelief she tamed the bad boy but she did.

At home, he knew there would be no cameras, no paparazzi. That was all his dad's doing because if it if it were up to Myriah, they would be in a banquet hall or hotel. It would be complete with a DJ, live music, catered food, and a huge dance floor. And lots of paparazzi. She did it all. She was his PR person, his "mamager", his editor when he made posts that she felt were inappropriate.

She was everywhere, following him to no end that it drove him nuts. Drove Mercedes nuts, too but they were stuck when it came to that. Ishmael "The Iceman" Payne was a brand and would forever be.

"You sure your girl's okay in there?" his boy Kevin asked, smiling. "Aunt Myriah still is not feeling her, my nigga. They stay calling us whores but scared ole girl is your match."

"How when I only bring around one girl? And she ain't' never seen me do anything," Ishmael said and snickered, thinking about the last time he snuck Teresita in and then Mercedes a few hours later.

He was glad those days were gone, sitting back as he grabbed him soda from the cooler. He wanted to smoke and sip on some Hennessey, but he would play it cool and respectful. Besides, he and his homeboys planned to turn up later on that night with all kinds of liquor on deck.

"I'm still shocked my damn self," Blooney, his other best friend asked, eyeing the patio door. He was waiting for his girl Cena to get there. She was a baddie, a Spanish bonita like Teresita. He'd been hitting her righteously for about three months, whenever and wherever. "Where's umm...Teresita" he asked and laughed. "We know you're still hitting the pussy."

Ishmael looked around quickly, gritting his teeth. "Yo, for real. Chill with that. And I don't know. I told her we was good."

"Before or after you fucked," Kevin asked.

"Fuck you, man," he said, waving them off. He would fuck Teresita if Mercedes didn't have the nose of three hound dogs, but he was good. He really did want to make it work and he felt like he was in love for the first time.

"After," Kevin and Blooney said simultaneously laughing as they dapped each other up.

"Too much pussy out here to be picking and sticking just one," Blooney said and grinned, watching a few girls who were there from the neighborhood. Since they all went to private school in the next county, cheating in the neighborhood was easy.

"So why Cena coming then?" Kevin asked his brother.

"Shit, why else? She's a freak. Couldn't wait until later on," he bragged, standing up as he rubbed the sea of waves on the top of his head.

A warm caramel complexion, Kevin was eye candy just like Ishmael. Standing at 6'3", lean yet cut, he easily got attention of grown women. Blooney, a bit buffer and darker, was the complexion of hot chocolate. Like his boys, he was undeniably sought out by many girls, standing at 6'4" with dreads and eight gold teeth. Four and the top and four at the bottom. He put the "h" in hood and wore them shits proudly.

"So why you messing with me? Terry ain't shit to me. Just familiar, that's all," he said when he really thought about it. Things with Mercedes were too good to be true at first, so he kept Teresita around not to feel stupid. But as time grew on, he felt in his heart Mercedes was the one. Just thinking about that good, good between her legs, made his jaw clenched as he sat back and eyed girl through the patio door.

Blooney too, talking crazy as he bricked up himself. "Bruh, next time pick a female that don't look like she's a beast in the sheets. Got damn." Ishmael shot him a look. "Shit, I'm saying though. She giving me a straight woody because my shit at attention," he laughed, dapping his Kevin up.

"Relax, yo. Don't think me letting you fuck Terry feel like Mercedes a toss around because she's not. Fuck wrong with you," he snarled, looking at Blooney as he sucked his teeth.

"True," Kevin said, agreeing with Ish but smiled as he whispered, "But she is finer as shit though. Got damn. Fam about to catch a charge for it, Bloon. Fuck a NBA."

"Imagine that," Ishmael said, rolling his eyes than laughed. "I am tripping, huh?"

"For real. I was just playing," Blooney said, smirking even though he wasn't. He shot Kevin a look that told him to just chill silently, shooting him a look back.

"You better. Ain't no way there would be ESPN and my name ain't mentioned," Ishmael bragged because he could. All the sports commentator called him "the Michael Jordan of the future" or "the new Lebron James". Especially now that they were in the state finals this year, seeking a third one.

Ishmael led them in all two and his senior year proved the third one would be a guaranteed state win. You couldn't turn on the television and not hear Ishmael Payne's name, dominating the county's school finals. His entire family, to include former crew members that used to work for Chico and Keyz, traveling from all over to watch him play.

Soon, Mercedes made her move once she showed him Teresita's hand. Surprisingly, instead of feeling like she was fake, he respected how she straight up told him she did it on purpose, knowing he deserved better. He figured she could have pretended it wasn't calculated, but respected how she showed her hand. She was beautiful, aggressive and his. Just like he wanted her to be.

Since she was old enough to drive, yet Big Wayne treated her like a princess, being dropped off and picked up by one of his men. He was out the game, but he wasn't dumb. He knew he would forever have enemies, making sure he protected his baby girl. She still, however, managed to get her first BMV at sixteen. But for now, she took advantage of riding in Ishmael's truck and on his dick.

As the three of them sat around and talked shit, waiting for the food to be served, Keyz, Chico, and their best friend, Skebo sat on the other side of the pool watching the younger version of themselves.

"You talk to him about what we discussed?" Chico asked Keyz, slowly sipping on an ice cold Corona. Even though Ishmael and Chico were well over the daddy/son issues once his paternity was confirmed, Keyz still had a way with Ishmael no one else had. Especially if it was a tough or touchy subject.

"Not yet, but I will. The boy's in love, Chico. Hell, we all know how that feels. I was a straight dummy, too busy out here chasing bids and dodging bullets. I used to see Iyana almost every fucking day when I first dropped out, mad as hell. But I wasn't focused."

Skebo laughed, remembering it like it was yesterday. "Nigger used to fuck anybody up he caught looking at her. I'm talking about he never would approach her, but let any dude even try to and this one would go straight looney on them. I keep telling everything this motherfucker right here the quiet yet psycho one."

"Ske, your bitch ass lying," Keyz shot back, smirking. "Not any dude. All them motherfuckers whether they looked at her or not. Even if they even looked past her, shit was getting knocked loose. Damn right," he said, his face all balled up.

They both laughed when he did, realizing Keyz was a true nut case about his wife. They couldn't be in the same house without him feeling the need to be near her or in her. Even if she was mad, she still had to give that ass up.

"He's not in love, though. He just thinks he is," Chico said lowly, leaning towards Keys. "You know how it is when you get the girl everybody shooting for. You feel like the man, that dude but the real man is the one that controls his own destiny, his own fate.

Once you give your heart away, even to the female you know is the one for you, everything you do and feel must revolve around her. Our boy is a top recruit, guaranteed to go first round in the NBA if his college career is a repeat of high school. That little girl right there is a recipe for disaster, I'm telling you," Chico said, watching his son.

Every two minutes, all Ishmael did was look back to see what Mercedes was doing. He made Myriah promise to be nice, but even if she was, he hated his son couldn't relax and enjoy his own time with his family.

"Well, no offense, but since your situation was kind of like that, maybe you would be more fit to speak on that," Skebo said, sort of addressing the elephant that popped up every now and again from their past.

"Seriously?" Chico asked Skebo, shaking his head.

"Hell yeah. Let's call that shit out. You would know."

"Bruh, I feel you, but I'm married now. Three kids later and my oldest damn near a celebrity. We did fucking good," he fumed, tossing his head back and he finished off his beer. "And slow your fucking road. My wife ain't—"

"Chill," Keyz said lowly, easing his hand between them.

He wasn't too proud he and his best friend used to be involved with the same woman, but it was what it was. He never loved Myriah. Never really cared to love her, but shit happens. He just didn't want it to happen again. "This is about my son. Less, a'ight," he said to the both of them.

"Whatever," Skebo, replied them both off. "I took that bullet," he tossed at them, remembering when Chico pumped a hot one in chest by accident back in the day. The crew was split in two, Keyz leading a group of them while Chico held most of the original members down. All over pussy, even though both would deny it before God.

"Ske, damn it, man. It was an accident," Chico told him, sucking his teeth. He almost shot his damn self when he shot Skebo by accident. He head was fucked up behind that, still was.

"I'm just saying, we all have fucked up back in the day. But that was serious, almost ended us," Skebo told them both. "I just don't want young Ish thinking with his dick. Put some eyes on her," he warned them. "With a mother like Paris, that fucking apple ain't falling too far," he said, remembering Paris sucking him off when he was a youngin' himself.

He was barely fifteen and Paris was letting him fall through every time he saw her in passing with a promise to break her off with something. Most times he did in exchange for some "neck" as he liked to call it.

"Some eyes?" Chico asked more so to himself, nodding his head.

"Hell yeah," Keyz said to himself, then reached over for some dap. "Good thinking, Ske. Who we putting on her."

"Naw, my boy not like us," Chico chimed in when he really thought about it. "Let's just play it cool for now. Myriah already doing too fucking much. Add our bullshit to the mix and he will cut us off. Nope, I saw we don't. Just for now."

"Yeah," Keyz said, agreeing. "Can't have him doing that."

"Alright then," Skebo said with a shrug as he grabbed a bottle of water.

"Bishop Ske not drinking today," Chico teased.

"Fuck you. Worry about your lose dick son and what he drinking," Skebo shot back and laughed.

"Shut your fertile ass up," Chico mumbled, looking around for his own kids. There was a gang of them. With he and Keyz's six, if you added Skebo's seven, they were already more than enough kids to start a basketball team.

"I'll be that," he winked, raising his bottle of water. "And three more coming."

"Bro, you really should get him and your sister checked out," Chico said to Keyz, knowing his sister Sunshine would do just that. Skebo always wanted a house full of kids and he was well on his way.

"Long as he keep them bad fuckers from around mine. Almost set my garage on fire," Keyz said, shooting Skebo a look.

By the end of the night, they all settled in and accepted that just like life had to teach them, it had to teach Ishmael too. Especially when they looked around and saw him gone. Him and his potential trapper called Mercedes

CHAPTER 5

*M*ercedes ran to the door, opening it without. She had just spoken to Ishmael, assuming it was him since they didn't see each other the night before. That was him when it came to *her*.

His girl.

His *Mercy*.

He was not the cold and callous person many encountered, especially on the court. No, with Mercedes, he was a doting, lovesick puppy sometimes, giving in to her. Even when she was in the wrong. If someone would've told him he was the settling down kind, he would call them a liar. But is Mercy had done that to him and now he was stuck. They had a beautiful senior year before graduation.

Right after, he whisked her way for a weekend to just be alone. Not only did they win as homecoming king and queen, but he won Most Likely to Succeed. Mercedes, however, won Most Likely to Not Get Married, pouting the entire day as the seniors swapped and signed yearbooks.

That trip was the first time he saw her even smiled. It only got better as they landed up in Orlando, than Daytona Beach enjoying long walks on the water, horse carriage rides, even a shopping sprees at a sleuth of high-end stores. Mercedes didn't want it to end as they approached the summer.

He would be off in two weeks for summer basketball camp and she would be in Miami plotting her next steps. That plan was a baby, then run her own clothing store complete with her own fashion line, *Mercy Me*. Of course, with is money.

Paris said that money from a man's account always felt better spent while you kept your own. So Mercedes was sticking to that. She just didn't know how soon her plans would come crashing down... and fast, leaving them both devastated.

§

"Oh, you!" she gasped, clutching the doorbell. "Petey. How are you?"

Petey, still every bit of boss raised by Big Wayne, his persona alone, took her breath away. Mercedes wanted to hate him, to reject him, but she couldn't. He was a package of "got damn" on sight, rendering her weak. He always was. Tall and dark, tatted up anywhere he could get a tat and smooth, his wardrobe staying on fly mode. Wearing a bald-head and full beard with sexy, full lips and lazy brown eyes, Petey had bitches lined up.

Even before he had money, working for when he couldn't go home or there was no home to go home to. A home that didn't come with much but had a steady flow of food, clothing, and lights on, now something of the past.

His mother fucked it all out, shooting shit up her arm or smoke it out of pipe. He didn't know if he wanted to love or hate Big Wayne who hired her, packaging everything from pills and crack to heroin. After a bad breakup with his father, instead of packaging the supply, she started using it and it was downhill from there.

The last he saw her, Petey he forced her to go to treatment. That was her third time, but something told him it would be her last, getting a call the night before she took off.

Moving past her, Petey walked in and turned around. He was

fucked up about his mother, but more importantly, that instead of wanting to go find her, he wanted Mercedes. Mercedes who was another man's girl.

He used to watch her get jealous, fuming whenever he had company over, figuring he deserved it once she linked up with Ishmael. That meant she couldn't stay out in the family room with him, watching television like they always did—talking in the wee hours in the morning like best friends.

The bitch's he brought around were light piranhas. They'd see her and instantly claimed their territory, dry humping until she was sick on her stomach as if they couldn't keep their hands off of him. She'd stomp off and wouldn't speak to him for days, even pretending to be sick so she wouldn't have to leave her room.

Petey loved Big Wayne like a father, never wanting to cross the line, but overtime, Mercedes proved she was worth crossing the line for and he's been gone ever since. He just couldn't wife her the way he wanted to, so she was playing with him by actually falling in love with Ishmael.

"The fuck you standing there for, ma? Close the door," he huffed, walking off to get him something to drink out the kitchen.

"Petey, what are you doing here?' she asked, walking quickly behind him. Ishmael had asked her once they every had a thing, but she denied it, knowing if Big Wayne ever found it, that would be the end of it for Petey. So they resorted to heated moments of bashing each other only to make up and not speak again for weeks at a time.

"Petey, I'm about to leave," she told him, standing at the kitchen door as he took his time. It was clear she was aggravated. Aggravated and even more....hurt. Hurt to the core, devastated but holding it up well. As well as she could as his lean body stood there in all of its goodness taunting her.

He had been ignoring her calls for weeks, ducking and dodging her when he stopped by. Even blocking her on social media. She was done. Done, done and he knew it too, gazing at her through his peripheral vision hoping she didn't pounce on him.

After he finished off a bottled water, he washed his hands, then grabbed a loaf of bread, turkey, ham, lettuce and cheese. He moved around the kitchen like he owned it, and her too which pissed her off even more.

"Are you for real?" she huffed, catching an attitude. "Just like that, you roll up in here and move around like it's okay, Petey?"

"Because it is okay, Mercedes. I fucking live here…right?" he said, a sly grin appearing on his face. His lips, lips she missed curl just a little forcing her to close her eyes.

Damn, him. Just damn him, she thought to herself.

"No, you *used* to. I have no clue where you lay your head these days," she painfully told him, quickly catching a tear. It never failed. Petey would get missing for weeks, whisking in and out of town for her father or God knows what else, then show up with no explanation.

She thought getting with Ishmael was a win/win. The first, proving to her mother and herself she could bag and baller. The second, more than that, was getting over Petey Jacobs.

What started off as a brother/ sister then best friend situation led to the first of many for her. The first kiss, touch between the fold of her legs, her first orgasm, her first love, her first heartbreak. All right under her parents nose. She hated him. Hated him so much, she loved him even more for making her do something no one else could.

That was care.

He glanced her way, taking a chunk of the sandwich into his mouth as he chewed slowly. So slow, his mind churned as he took in the one person that made him do stupid shit. Stupid shit like fuck other women and waste money just to not think about her.

He kept telling himself she was a bougie, pampered chick that was his boss's daughter. She was born into money. He had to rob and kill to get his and he'd be damned he let love stop him.

But it did…

Especially when the blogs flooded his timeline and boy were they generous. Everyone he logged into had a headliner about Miami's sensational, star point guard, Ishmael Payne. He was everyone, dripping all over from what he wore to what he had in his mouth. It didn't help he also was the son of the infamous kingpin, Chico Ramos. Or Keyz Payne depending on which story you believed.

Ishmael was an animal, a beast on the court and in the streets, motherfuckers respected him. He did, too. He wasn't hating because Ishmael was rich or was talented. He was hating because he stole his girl.

His girl. She belonged to him.

"Funny you should say that," he said and laughed, grabbing a glass to pour him something to drink. "I heard you have plans to lay your head somewhere. Traveling soon? Or better yet, relocating?" he probed, giving her the evil eye. His eyes dark, flooded with pain. He couldn't understand why she just wouldn't' be with him, making things worse as she gave the paparazzi something to talk about.

"If you mean on campus at Flo Mo," she said, referring to the local college just north of where she lived. "Then yes."

"That's your word, ma?" he laughed and shook his head, sliding her his cell. "I just want to make sure the shit that's popping is all bullshit. But here, look around."

Fumbling, she held it in her, squinting as she scrolled through a sleuth messages. They were between her and her best friend, Christian. As she read them, swiping frantically, her face grew red.

"How did you get these?" she growled lowly, clenching her fist as she held onto the cell tightly. They were an exchange of text messages that spoke of her plans to move to Durham with Ishmael.

"The how don't fucking matter," he said, his voice laced with venom. A chill felt in the room he created, boring into her eyes. "What the hell is that, Mercedes? Really?" he said, his voice cracking before he cleared it. He was upset and more—hurt. Yes, she saw hurt and that, whether he knew it or not, hurt her more.

If anyone knew of the nightmares he endured, the days he went without just to get by, she did. She never once felt sorry for him, instead welcoming him in their home. He was like a live in playmate, older though. Cuter too, and he liked. He liked her a lot and she liked him too.

"When this happened, I—I was upset. You were at that strip club, doing God's knows what with...the women, the money. Just acting like we are nothing, Petey. I get it, I swear I do. I'm Big Wayne's daughter, but when is enough enough?" she poured out, her body shaking.

It had been almost six months since he held a decent conversation with her. Six months and all she wanted to do what be held by him, told he wouldn't ignore her and leave again like that.

"Ugh, I hate you!" she screamed, charging his way as she pushed him in his chest. "You don't get to make me feel bad! Nope, you don't," she said once more, out of breath as she pushed him away.

"Naw, princess. Don't flip this shit on me. You don't get to forget you pushed me away, " he hissed, walking up on her. "You just hate you can't always have your way, Mercedes. I was ready, ready to tell Big Wayne, but naw, you worried about what Paris thinks. Don't fucking play the victim, ma. Shit's fucked up enough, my baby."

"So she could sabotage you? You know her," she said, looking around as if her mother was there. She wasn't. She'd slipped off to some island on a cruise. Mercedes was sure it wasn't with her girl-friends, but that was Paris. She did her thing and Big Wayne did his.

She didn't want that life for herself, her fists balled up as she wanted to hit Petey for making her feel anything.

"How, baby? For loving you? For wanting to right by you? Mercedes, I'm busting my ass for your dad, opening new restaurants, bars, handling his business. Shit, I even picked up a side hustle for you," he told her, grabbing her firmly her by both wrists. "Don't do this," he pleaded.

"Move," she fussed, trying to wiggle away. "You don't get to tell me what not to do. Ugh!" He laughed, pulling her closer to him. His breath, warm and minty tickled her nose. He kissed her mouth once and hard, as she shoved him away.

"No, stop it! Just stop it," she growled as he kissed her even more. Her resolve gave way as his kisses slowed down, pressed her mouth longer, more passionate. Her cries met with a quiet no, sucking softly and gently on her lips as he shook his head no.

"I can't stop. I just can't," he confessed, pulling away as he stroked her cheek lightly. Without thinking, her head leaned into it. His rough hands felt like pillows. Pillows that gave her rest… in him.

Sighing, he sighed too amazed he still nabbed this girl. "So fucking beautiful… and I hate you, too," he whispered and lied, his teeth pinching his bottom lip. He loved her, but hated she had that kind of power over him. He climbed out of pussy as soon as he saw those text messages, coming all the way from Palm Beach to get there.

He might have been mad, ready to kill her but he was scared too. He didn't want to lose her. He couldn't.

"Don't stop fighting for us," he asked softly, pinching her chin.

She dropped her head, turning it when he caught it with his mouth. "Don't," he said once more against her lips. He wrapped her in his arms, indulging in the sweetest thing he's ever tasted. Her. Her completely. Everything about her was sweet.

The kiss—it was warm, slow, and wet. Just like her juices that now flowed for him. His tongue now wrapping around hers, in and out followed by small pecks.

"No," she whimpered in between kisses. "I hate—" she started but stopped he went in, licking, sucking, pulling, begging and all.

"Let him go, baby. Please, let him go. I got you. That money don't mean shit without being with me."

"But—" she tried to reply, but failed terribly as he slipped his hands under her ass. His face crashing against her neck.

"So soft," he said just above a whisper, sniffing and tasting it as he licked it slowly. "And sweet."

She wanted him to stop, needed him to but she couldn't reject him. He was like a drug, a magnet, an addiction. They both were for each other. They knew it, too.

They hadn't fucked in months, so he wasn't stopping now. Not even if God himself came down and told him to. His rebellious soul and hunger for her just wouldn't let him. He tried fighting it all these months, but that text saying she was leaving and with another man him was it.

"Wait," she said, stopping him abruptly. "You fucking Christian?" She was serious too, gripping his hardened member as he laughed.

"Yo, girl. Stop. I'm trying to get in your pussy."

"I'm serious, Petey. Are you?" She was holding her breath, never trusting anyone. Not even Christian, even she did have her own stable of men. She was fast beyond her years, a reason they connected and pretty, if not prettier than her. Her parents pill heads with boatloads of money, running a chain of drug stores in some of the roughest part of town.

"Fuck no. Let's just say she don't even know I got her cell. Forward them shits to myself," he said with a shrug. "Y'all rich chicks don't care. Just like fuck it, I'll get a new one," he laughed, watching her squint her eyes as if she didn't believe him.

"Mango, huh?" she asked, speaking of his homeboy that fucked with Christian from time to time.

"I plead the fifth," he laughed, roughing her up as he snatched her to him. "Don't play. You trying to get off the subject. Durham, Mercedes? It's just that easy to leave me? I thought we had a deal."

"Pfft, a deal? What part of deal was you fucking a gang of women, Petey? Not one, but unlimited bitches!" she snapped as he refused to let her go.

"Mostly, business movies and bitches will be bitches," he growled lowly in her ear. "And I wasn't fucking them..." he said, his voice trailing off as he leaned back. "Well, not all of them. Neck maybe, but baby, I swear it wasn't like that."

"Ugh, you lie so much! Move! Move, got damnit!" She snatched away quickly, wiping her mouth. "Nope. I'm not doing this with you. Besides, it's too late!" she told him with a smile. It was evil, watching him fume as she did. "You see the headlines. I'm like celebrity famous."

"Celebrity famous, with a local basketball kid? Really?" he said, chewing on the inside of his jaw. He knew he was being petty, but so what? So was she.

"Who is getting major looks," she said, grinning as she crossed her arms and rubbing it in. "His mother, even though I can't stand that bitch, is making sure he is. So yes, celebrity."

"So that's all you want to be known for? A basketball wife bitch while he's on the road fucking God knows who?"

"How is that any different than you wanting to be hood famous? Huh?" she asked, rolling her neck with one hand on her hip. "Tell me, Petey because I'm all ears. As far as I was concerned, you're the one who moved on. Ain't that right? How many calls you ignored? Text messages?"

"If I did, then why am I here?" he asked, gripping her by the neck. She gasped, forcing him to loosen his grip just a little but he was angry, pissed she didn't remember she forced him out there.

"Pet—"

"Naw, this is what you wanted. Everyday I do what I do for us. To show you when you ready for me, that I got us. So we can have our own shit. Not Big Wayne's, not Paris's. The fuck you mean I moved on? I'm setting myself up and you, Miss Lady, have gotten way too got damn comfortable. Nigger all on the Gram talking about Cedes, baby this and Cedes, baby that. Fuck him. End that, ma and I mean that shit," he growled lowly.

His eyes traveled down, admiring all that goodness in front of him. She was wearing an acid washed, denim top that hung off her shoulders, skinny distressed jeans, and grey Pumas. Ishmael loved Pumas, buying her a pair each time he bought himself a pair which made Petey growl.

"I should make you take them bullshits off. Fucking Pumas. Bum as shoes. And all your clothes," he whispered harshly, lifting his head as he dared her to talk back. She didn't, fighting hard to hold in the smile his crazy brought out of her. She loved that looney shit, never seeing it with Ishmael. Not like this.

Yeah, she was addicted to him... all of him.

"What are you going to do about it, huh?" she asked, taunting him. You wanted him to take her, do what he wanted with her.

That was Petey. He was rough, but she liked it with her. Especially when it came to fucking. She grinned, enticing him—silently begging him to have his way. She loved Ishmael, but she was *crazy in love* with Petey.

It didn't have to make sense to anyone she resolved within herself, willing him with her eyes to just have his way as he made his move.

"Damn you," she whispered, her chest heaving up and down as he dragged one index finger down then around one nipple. He pinched it and let it go, stepping back as he released her throat. She opened her mouth, touching her neck. She missed his touch just that quickly, wanting his hands all over her.

He saw the disappointment in her face, leaning down to look in her eyes. When he did, a curl fell. He grabbed it and twirled it around his finger, mind fucking her. He knew his girl. She could be bougie and selfish, but not when it came to him.

They were Petey and Mercedes. Unstoppable, ready to claim his girl as soon as her parents walked in the door. He gently tucked it behind her ear, relishing in it's texture. It was soft, just like her.

"I love this shit," he told her, a faint smile appearing. "Everything about you, but especially this. Our kids would have good fucking hair," he laughed, rubbing his low fade. Hers was long. Long and thick, wand curls lying loosely around her shoulders. "My shit is—"

"Perfect, just like you," said Mercedes, interrupting him. "To me you are just that." His eyes landed her lips. Gosh, he could get lost in them. Glistening from the nude lip-gloss, he imagined them wrapped firmly around his dick.

"Oh yeah?" was all he said, wishing he was inside of her. He grimaced, thinking about Ishmael fucking her the way she did him. She started out slow, but she caught on fast. Everything she did in the bedroom or anywhere for that matter, he taught her. He knew ever nook and cranny on her body, his name tatted in Arabic above her rather round derriere. Ishmael was told it meant peace, being none the wiser.

He knew Petey was Muslim, but not a practicing one. Neither was Big Wayne, even though sometimes he would go to Friday prayer also known as Jumu'ah. He found Allah after almost being killed, which started his journey out the game.

"Have to be for you, Mercedes," he said, his fingers traveling the letters of his name.

"Then why are we going through this? The games? Other people?"

"Because you're fucking playing me," he snarled lowly, walking up on her. "None of that had to be our story. I did that to stop myself from hating you, for you pushing me away. Then to go get some pussy ass ….Argghh," he grunted, clenching his fists.

"Only after you played with me first. It was supposed to be a front, not factual," she responded like a little kid.

"Mercedes, this is not recess. Not a little game. This is fucking life. My life, yours too," he told her, his voice croaking. "I'm tired, baby. Can we just stop now."

That did it, sending a river down as her eyes filled up like a flood. Mercedes, always the emotional one, couldn't believe he was emotional today. She kept telling herself she was done with Petey, now here he was making her get all in her feelings and for doing what she knew was true. That was telling the truth.

"You don't want me," she said, baiting him to say the opposite. She needed to hear that, anything now to get him to say it but he said more.

"Shorty, I would die for you," he said, his voice still. So still, it shook her to the core. His eyes locked in, not moving. Caramel brown orbs that seeped into a dark, cedar color as he dropped his head. " I would bury bitches for you," he confessed. "So that's it. I'm telling."

"But daddy…"

"I know, baby," he said and sighed. "But I'm a man. Big Wayne knows that. He has to let me be one, even if that means fucking his daughter. I can't lie, you're like the forbidden fruit, more than a fucking apple. The whole garden, Mercedes. A garden he controls. I owe him everything, but I can't keep pretending that garden is now mine. Neither should you."

"Who says I am I'm pretending?" she mumbled, feeling guilty because a part of her was doing just that—pretending. Ishmael looked good to the world, but Petey felt like home. Home to her heart.

"Me," he said, pinching her chin as he held up it. "So wrap that shit up. Let his ass go since he got that letter, baby. He has a lot to look forward to and me too. With you though."

"To do exactly what, Petey? You're ready to finally commit? I admit it was my idea but it was to save your ass. You needed to survive.

Messing with me wasn't a way to do that. Trust, anything I ever did was for you."

"I'm ready, ma. I swear. I've been ready."

She leaned into his touch, inhaling his scent, which was woody but also smelled like soap. ""Just give me some time. I promise you, it will be like old times soon but better. No hiding then."

Petey stretched his eyes, still not content with that answer. Neither was she, but one thing's for sure was their familiarity with each other. They could talk for hours, lie up, and look at the stars with his rooftop on his truck open, smoking a blunt. Petey had dreams, big dreams but he was getting impatient, waiting on Mercedes.

The blogs snapped him out of it and quick. He was almost there, secretly linking up with Chello, the last original OG that ran The Crew. Petey wanted big money and fast, pushing guns which was something Chello had his hands into. Dope was good, but guns were better. You could move a load faster and quieter. Especially when he was married to the DEA, his wife.

"More time?" he asked, pulling her to him. She flinched, shaking her head as she closed her eyes.

"Petey, baby?"

"Fuck, I can't touch you now?" he asked softly, taking a deep breath. "You don't love me no more, baby?" he whispered, watching her chest rise and fall as he lowered his head.

He applied light pecks, pulling her to him as he gripped her ass cheeks. She smelled so fucking good. She could barely contain herself, she felt her center thumping as he leaned her head back. Neither could he, groping both breasts as his mouth found hers. He was a skilled lover, a patient one too but not today. He hadn't felt her pussy in a minute, eager to slide inside of her warm, wet walls.

❧

*O*n the other side of town was Ishmael. He was about to hop in his truck to go and picked her up. It was a surprise though. Something he had planned special for her before leaving off for school. The summer was quickly approaching and she was getting moody. He knew it was about the distance, but today he was sealing the deal. He wasn't proposing, but he did have something to prove he was all the way in.

A promise ring.

A buzz, however, from his cell, got his attention before he backed out.

"Damn, who is this?" he said to himself confused, looking at his screen. It was a text from an unfamiliar number, telling him to get to Mercedes's house and fast. "Go to Mercedes's house?"

Strangely, he called her cell multiple times but she never picked up. Pulling up, he pulled out his pistol and jotting up the stairs.

"What? Huh?" he asked himself as he stopped midway in the living room. "Is somebody fucking?"

He felt the floor moved, the gasps, the groans and moans sounding just like his woman. "Man, hell naw."

By then, the drive, the need to hurt someone for her was gone. His arm that held his piece, dangled loosely as he took a slow painful walk following the sounds all the way to the kitchen.

Then he saw her... and him. His mouth agape, his feet stuck to the floor. It was like a nightmare, a fucking horror story as he felt her his heart ripped out of his chest. By then, Petey had bent down and lifted Mercedes on the kitchen counter, her ass spread out as he prepared to eat her for lunch.

"You still fucking with me, Mercedes? We still in this together no matter what?" he asked her, pulling her jeans off that hung on one foot. He planted kisses, starting from her ankle up her thigh. "Please, baby. Please don't do this to us," he growled, Mercedes's face flushed with passion as she bit her lip.

"Yes, baby. Oh yes," she uttered. The more she bit on her lip, the angrier he became. They were so into it, neither knew there lives were on the line until they heard a sound that usually indicated that.

Click, click.

"What that—"

"Shut your bitch ass up," Ishmael growled, resting the mouth of the gun against Petey's temple. "And you? Really bitch?" he asked, gritting his teeth.

"It's not—It's not—"

"It's exactly what the fuck I think it is," he said, his hand shaking. Petey was ready to snatch his from his hip, knowing this wouldn't end well. Ishmael's was Chello's nephew or like one, unsure where Mercedes's loyalty lied.

"You love him?" he asked her, then pushed the mouth of the pistol harder when Petey flinched. "Don't or this bitch will be painted in red, my guy. Fucking red."

"Hey, she was mine—"

"Petey, no!" Mercedes called out, pleading with him to shut up. "Just don't. Please…"

"Do you love him?" he asked her again, his voice shaking. He had only cried once behind a woman—his mother. She betrayed him by loving two men. And now, it seemed like Mercedes was doing the same. *Why God? Why me*, he asked himself as he looked up at the ceiling, then quickly back down at Petey. "Fuckkkkk!" he screamed, hitting Petey across the head.

"Argghh," he belted, holding his head. All Petey saw was death, ready to assassinate him. "Damn, my nigga. Fuck," he whispered, wiping the blood that seeped out of his scalp.

"Ishmael," she said lowly, reaching down to put back on her jeans until he stopped her.

"Naw, don't," he said and laughed. "Let this fuck boy finish it up. Shit, or not. It really don't matter to me," he told her, his eyes now dark and still. "Because fuck it, it's over," he told her, tossing the box on the ground.

He was ready to body both of them, but he remembered the conversation he had with Keyz and Chico just the other night. It was like God rewinding back time long enough for him to do the right thing.

That was leave and leave now.

"If she's really yours son, you will know sooner than you think. Distance

helps you figure that out," Chico said to him, glad Mercedes was staying in Miami.

"Distance is just that, dad. Distance," he said with a shrug as he popped a fry in his mouth. They were at Cheeks, his aunt Iyana's restaurant. Well, one of them since she had three. "We got that figured out," he told them, eager to get Mercedes to North Carolina as soon as he could.

"How sure are you?" Keyz asked, looking at Chico.

"Sure about what, pops?" he asked Keyz.

"That you have that all figured out. You have plans, solid plans but she's just doing what, waiting on you to wish rings and shit and become the misses?"

"Pops, come on now. She's going to school, doing her fashion thing too."

"With our money," Chico chimed in, shaking his head.

"With my money," Ishmael told him.

"Money we made sure you had...get our point," Keyz said. "One thing about my wife, your auntie is she never let me give her anything. She was a boss in her own right. She went to college, started teaching dance classes, then built her own community center using county funds and her own money. Even when we got together, she barely took my shit," he said and laughed, remembering how he had to go behind her back to pay for things.

"And your mother, too," Chico said, hoping to drill their point on home. "When she stopped fucking with me, she got her shit together. Got her a degree, started teaching and bought y'all her first house. Her ass barely let me step my black ass inside," he laughed, remembering how hard he had to work to get Myriah back.

"Where is all this going?" Ishmael quizzed them both, eyeing them suspiciously.

Keyz leaned forward, hoping his son was really listening. If not, they would have to turn it up a notch. Especially since Skebo already sent enough footage on Petey and Mercedes. He and Chello were pretty tight, attending bible study together. No matter how deep Chello was still in the game, marriage and fatherhood had him almost bribing God.

Skebo would ride with him from time to time, recognizing Petey when he used to be out there with Big Wayne. Once Keyz and Chico gave him the nod to put eyes on Mercedes, he sadly learned that she wasn't shit but a headache waiting to happen and a body or two to pop if Big Wayne came for Ishmael for fucking her up.

"A real woman never takes. She grinds for her own. Now a bitch, she takes, thinking pussy gives her the right to. But the kicker is, pussy is between every bitch's legs. A hustle is not. If she's using your money as her hustle by way of pussy, distance only means she's hustle the same fucking way while you're gone."

"Shit, or while you're not around," Skebo said, stepping up and taking a seat as he gave them both a subtle nod.

"Pops? Dad? Y'all know something I don't know because yo, all this riddle talk got me confused."

"Don't be confused young blood," Skebo said. "Be careful. Sometimes you have to move silently and announce your every move. Especially when its you taking all the risks."

"Don't announce every move, huh?"

"Naw, don't. Most times, the answer is right in front of you. Now, if you two old motherfuckers tired of schooling Ish, I'm ready to eat. Sunshine and my got damn kids been gone all day. That means no dinner for my black ass," Skebo said, waving Iyana over.

"Hey you. I got all of you up here this evening. Ish, you're okay?" she asked her nephew who appeared to be in deep thought.

"Yeah, auntie. I'm straight," he said, pushing his chair back as he stood up. "I got a lot to do over the next few days," he said, dapping them all up. He reached over and gave his aunt a kiss on the cheek. "Love you, auntie. I'll holler."

"Son, just think about what we said," Chico cautioned him, hoping he really di.

"For sure..."

Ishmael replayed that conversation over and over. He could lose it all or he could have it all.

He chose to have it all. Just without her.

In the meantime, Keyz and Chico were waiting for an update. "He's there?" they asked Chello who was on speakerphone, parked across the street.

"Yeah and leaving. He don't look too good either. I got him. Just be prepared. Once a man heart turns cold, it takes time and the right woman to fix it," he told them. "If that's even possible."

"And what about Petey?" Chico asked, ready to fuck him up.

"What about him? Love makes you do dumb shit sometimes, right?" Chello asked, waiting for him to contest.

He didn't as he sighed. Myriah was proof of that everyday.

"Yeah, you're right, my man. You're motherfucking right."

"He'll heal. Trust me."

Keyz and Chico looked at each other. They had healed, but Ishmael wasn't like them. They were savages, unable to love for a long time until they did. They just hated this time Myriah was right.

Mercedes wasn't good enough for their son.

She was another Myriah.

CHAPTER 6

JUNE 2019

"*C*an you please go get your sister?" Chico asked Iyana, watching Myriah at a distance as they sat in the truck. They all drove up to see Ishmael off. It was six weeks before classes started, and all the freshman basketball players had to report in for orientation and basketball camp.

He'd been distant with them all, not even sharing why he abruptly cut things off with Mercedes. The blogs were vicious, calling him a future whore. Myriah was furious, but he remained true to himself.

Instead of dogging Mercedes out, he took the high road and only stuck with one script. That's to be the best the NCCA and then NBA would ever see. He didn't want to be the next Dwayne Wade, Michael Jordan anything.

He wanted to be Ishmael "The Iceman" Payne and he did that shit well already. He refused to walk around sulking, pushing his feelings back. He was done with bitches and he prayed he was done with them. Like his court name, that's who he was now—cold.

Even cursed he ex Teresita out, seeing posts on IG about the "IT" team. That "Ish and Terry" were back together again. All that did was send Mercedes into a nutcase, posting her own lies about why they weren't together.

Some days before he left, he didn't even go home, camping out at Keyz and Iyana's house instead. There, he could just relax, be himself. With his mother, he had to be great all the time and he was sick of it. She was all too happy he was single, while his father seemed to know it was more. He just wouldn't speak on it.

That was Chico. He'd fucked up so much in the past, he just let Myriah have her way. So she did and everyone was paying for it.

"I'll try, but I can't promise you anything," Iyana said, slipping out the back door as she shook her head. She stopped and poked her head inside of the passenger window before she took off. "If you see me pulling her, dragging her on the ground, just come and help me. I swear she was like this his first day of pre-K and Kindergarten."

Chico remembered, watching far off since no one knew he was his father. Myriah cried in his arms all day the first time Ishmael went to pre-K. He lost money that day, but nothing would make him not be there for his son then or now. That was his fuck up he caused, so he was all in until they got it right.

"She won't. Ish won't let her do that. His teammates will straight clown on him if he does. Just be gentle with her. She's been snapping on me the entire fucking trip."

"I know, but he's still her baby. Now," she said, patting his arm. "Wish me luck."

As she made her way across the lawn to them, Keyz couldn't wait to get Chico alone. Their son had not been himself and he wasn't feeling it at all. He understood how it was to be played, ready to put some hands on a few people, starting with Mercedes.

"Aye, Mercedes came by before we left, looking for Ish at the restaurant."

"Word?"

Chico knew it had to be God she didn't come to their house, playing victim. They only reason she was even still breathing was because of his son. Even though he didn't fuck with her anymore, he knew Mercedes still had his son wide open. Only a man with a broken heart acted they way Ishmael was acting. He was hitting every strip club too, the blogs eating it up.

"Yeah, but you know Iyana. Always the nurturing one, being sweet and shit. I spoke, but made it clear she can't come around there. Ish was fucked up, yo."

"We need to handle her?" Chico asked him, suggesting more than what he said.

"Boy, we not about that life anymore," Keyz laughed then stopped, watching his son struggle to say goodbye. "Fuck," he muttered, wanting to step out and to go him. "My son. My fucking son," he growled lowly, gritting his teeth.

"Our son," Chico corrected him, sucking his teeth. "Look at him," he said, watching his body relax when Myriah hugged and kissed him on the top of his head. "A fucking baby, yo."

"Yeah, but he's amazing," Keyz said. "Better than us, much better."

"Keyz—"Chico started to say then stopped.

"I know, man. I know." They had this conversation at least every six months, how Keyz was the one to really hold Ishmael down. The one who taught him to be a man, to be responsible. The one who put a ball in his hand. "And stop being hard on yourself. You stepped up. Both of y'all did. This just a fucking phase, man. A phase. We both had them."

"A phase?"

"Hell yeah. Thank God for that shit. Don't forget all those nights your old ass slept on my sofa, corn fritter, smelling toe nigger when Myriah put your ass out," Keyz teased.

"Fuck you," Chico snapped back, then laughed. "Yeah, I was, huh? Her ass fucked up all my shit. Fucking wanna be Stella ass," he laughed.

"Hell yeah, but love changes the lens on a lot of shit. His will when it's time. It had to happen. Now it's our job to make sure he stays focused," Keyz schooled him.

"How, man?"

"How what?"

"How you get so damn in tuned with women and God?"

"That woman right there," Keyz said, pointing to his wife. "Before, her, I was a damn fool. I had bitches, money, cars and shit I couldn't even name, but I was empty. For years I was until her."

"Word?" Chico said, wondering why he and Myriah were still fucking up. They had to be if Ishmael was still making the wrong moves.

"Oh, and the word. I'm no Skebo," Keyz laughed. "I hit church up at least on the first Sunday, pay my tithes and pray. I learned it works, bro. It really works."

"Yeah, and look at your wife. A hundred dollars she'll be crying next. Teddy bears."

"She my teddy bear, fool. But if she is, her ass better not be pregnant. With Cree whining ass, Kaison the baby who ignores her, crying is a sign another baby is on the way."

"This lying motherfucker," Chico mumbled, cranking the trunk up. "Your tender-hearted ass would jump at another baby."

"You right," Keyz laughed. "I am lying. Look at my baby," Keyz whispered and smiled, opening the back door as he got out. "Come to daddy, baby. Stop all that crying," he said as she hugged Ishmael, quickly running his way.

"Stop," she laughed, dabbing both eyes with the back of her hand while Myriah went over to Chico.

"Is he going to be okay?" Myriah asked her husband.

Chico looked her in the eye, meaning every word that he was about to speak to her. He'd been a fuck up since they day they met, her too if they both were being honest, but that same child she was crying over was their strength. They had to be strong for him since it was him that kept all four of them together over the years.

"With parents like us and he *still* made it, of course, baby. Why wouldn't he?" he assured her, giving his son a nod who looked their way.

He mouthed, "I love you" and when he did, Ishmael pumped his chest twice and nodded. Chico's heart swelled up just a little more when he did because truthfully Ishmael's existence is what made him a real man.

Not street credibility, bitches, or material things. It was his son.

CHAPTER 7

*I*shmael entered his apartment suite designated for athletes. There were two athletes in each one, something he wasn't used to. That was sharing his personal space. Even with having a gang of younger siblings and cousins, Ishmael was spoiled, always having his own. But like life that seemed to change overnight, so was his attitude. This was it for now, so he decided to roll with it.

After putting his cell on the charger, he took a walk back into the living room to gather the rest of his things.

"This woman," he huffed, looking at two sets of towels in almost every color that existed under the sun. "Doing too much," he said and laughed as he looked at four comforter sets. Even though the university had a cafeteria just for athletes, Myriah went a step further, purchasing all kinds of pots and pans, silverware, a crock-pot and air fryer.

She had it shipped, meeting them in the parking lot inside of a pod. He wanted to be angry, feeling like she was suffocating him but he couldn't lie, she did make him feel loved.

Love—he hated that fucking word.

He eventually took a seat on the sofa, resting his body. He had to be up at four AM, but only had put half of things away. Just when he dozed off, the front door opened.

"Ishmael 'The Iceman' Payne!" he heard, rubbing his eyes as he sat up. "When they told me I would be living with you, I was like hell naw! I'm Reno. Well, Jason but they call me Reno the Rhino, you know because I'm big and shit. Oh, and from Nevada."

And was huge he was, broad shoulders and neck. He was a Shaq in the making, standing easily at 6'8". Peanut butter color skin, a light fade, and baby-like face with full cheeks and bushy eyebrows. His feet were easily a size fifteen.

The weather was in the sixties, colder than what either was used to. While Ishmael had on a red and white Polo zip up jacket and sweats, Reno was where Nike basketball shorts and a t-shirt that tightly hugged his body. Although big, Reno was light on his feet, a force to be reckoned with as the leading center from out the west coast.

Ishmael smiled as he stood. Just like his name was known around the nation for NCCA picks to go that schools had to have, so was Reno's. He may have been from the west state, but he looked like a healthy, well-fed country boy from the south. And he should since his mother was from Mississippi.

"Man, that's what's up," Ishmael said, adjusting his eyes as the room was darker than it was earlier. He had to have been sleep for a few hours, noticing the sun had set. "Shoot, I fell asleep. And thanks for the love. Reno, the damn Rhino, huh," he said, mimicking the sports commentators because of Reno's size. "Let me go wash up right quick."

Ishmael grabbed a washcloth from his room, went into the bathroom, and washed his face. He grabbed his toothpaste and toothbrush too, feeling hungry. He low key hoped Reno was hungry too, so they could step out. If not, he was about to put something on his stomach. He wasn't too fond of cafeteria food, but he might slide through to see what they had up in there once he looked at what came with his scholarship.

"I don't know about you, but man, I can eat!" Reno said to him and smiled, watching Ishmael rubbed his stomach.

"You saw that, huh?" he laughed. "Muhfucka starving. I was glad my moms left, but right about now..."

"I know, man," he agreed, rubbing the top of his head. "I could sit around and order in, waiting for my stuff to get here, but let's hit it. My stuff got on the wrong plane. Too damn big to sit on the first one, so they switched me to first class on a different plane. My suitcase just didn't follow. But I guess this it until tomorrow," he said, pointing to a carry on. "That first flight was fucking my knees up!" he laughed.

Ishmael knew exactly how he felt, often having to adjust where he sat in a restaurant because of his height. Even his bed at home was a custom order due to his height. As for flying, Myriah was on point. She always made sure his was first class or the emergency exit row, but even that was too tight depending on the airline.

He could tell Reno was easy going, a talker who would talk without much prompting. He needed that so he wouldn't think about Mercedes. He was a ticking time bomb, now blocking her on every site, cell phone and email. He listened to one of her messages that broke his heart and left a hole in his wall. One he didn't care to explain to no one.

"I'm ready," he told Reno, deciding to leave his cell. When he stepped outside, the cool breeze hit his face and he exhaled. He looked around, taking the scenery in. It was no Miami, but he was glad it wasn't.

Home represented failure to him. All he had now going for him was basketball, so he was ready to fuck a hoop up on the court first chance he got.

❧

*P*epper had been up since six AM. She had to get her siblings up, make sure they bathed, were dressed, and fed before the morning school bus came and left them. Living on a side of town they did, they already didn't have the best schools, but their public bus system wasn't the best either. So, anything to make sure they got to school was a must.

After a few times, Pepper became a drill sergeant, waking Drew and Bryce up who'd probably stayed up half the night quietly playing videos game. Even shoving them in and out of the bathroom as she ironed their clothes.

When she was done, she'd start a pot of oatmeal, maybe throw in a few slices of bacon, boil a few eggs and toast if they had any to keep them full until lunch time. No matter what, Pepper refused to let her siblings step out hungry and unkempt.

They were already young black men, easily targeted depending on what they wore. So she braided their hair down at least once a week after washing it, refusing to allow them to grow dreads.

"Girl, did you sleep last night?" Sashay asked her. They met years ago in the hood, excited when they both got the athletic cafeteria. Sashay so she could meet the players and ditch her deadbeat baby daddy, Pepper so she could get a signed t-shirt or jersey for her brothers. They loved sports, often asking her who she had seen on campus that's on TV. She had only been there a month, looking for a job all summer long after graduating

Before then, Sashay was a booster, stealing and selling clothes like hot cakes. She had the best of wardrobes, living a hood royalty life except her baby daddy wouldn't let her. Anything she brought in, he stole, so working a real job was more her speed as she found a way to get rid of him.

Pepper was just glad to have something stable, and something that had a gang of overtime.

"No, did you sleep? You're the one with the man," Pepper said, shooting her a look.

"That bitch. Girl, no," she said, rolling her eyes. "Right now he is a glorified babysitter for Fat Fat," she said, speaking of their son.

"I did, I guess. Grabbed a Red Bull which seems to be working. And you know we will be here all day. They can eat I heard," Pepper laughed.

She actually enjoyed watching people eat, cooking for them too.

When she did, life seemed to pass by but in a way that eased her mind. She relished in the laughs and chatter, remembering brief moments when it was like that at home. Times when her mother was really a mother.

Just yay tall, Carrie would have Pepper standing on a stool, seasoning and stirring a pot a collard greens to whipping up a batch of cornbread batter for Carrie's infamous corn casserole cornbread. They kept a line coming until there was nothing left to make.

Pepper was smart too, interested in getting a degree in business but for now that was just a dream. Reality was getting a check, paying rent and keeping the lights on. It took discipline, but she was committed to doing just that. She deserved better, but her brothers more.

They already had two strikes against them, being males and black. Add a third one if a absent father was added into the equation. All she knew was they wouldn't be a statistic. Well, not a new one since they already were.

She watched everything from Rachel Ray to Martha Stewart and Snoop Dog. She wanted to start her own cooking show, introducing ethnic dishes that could be incorporated globally. Her dreams were big, but for now, she was focusing on getting this check.

If she had to fight her own mother, there was no way she was fighting a bitch on campus about her college dude to lose her job. Her motto was to smile, dump food on the tray, pour a drink if they asked for refills and to keep it moving. All in that order.

As Ishmael and Reno took a slow walk to the cafeteria, they became acquainted with each other. Reno couldn't believe they both had seven younger siblings. Ishmael spared him the story about having two fathers that contributed to those kids. Not that he gave a fuck, but being too friendly too soon could cost you and he wasn't all the way right in his head just yet.

He still loved Mercedes, but hated her too. So, of course, when the subject of having a girl came up, Ishmael moved around it and gave a bullshit ass answer.

"Fuck them hoes," he drawled, then shot a smile Reno's way.

"Exactly!" he said, cosigning it. "I had to cut them all loose. Too much to sample right here, you know what I mean?" he said, casting his eyes at two girls who just passed them, smiling and waving.

"Well, you sample. I'm straight for now. Moms didn't even want me up here thinking I would get some lost in some pussy."

"Yeah? You had it like that back home? Bitches coming through and fucking in the house?"

"Let's just say I wasn't missing out on anything moving. I did my thing, but hey, time to focus on some new shit. Fuck them hoes."

"I feel you, Ice! Fuck 'em," Reno quickly, dapping him up, causing Ishmael to bust out laughing.

"Your ole country ass."

"My country ass can fuck some shit up on the court, too. Protect your ass if I have to. Fuck what you saying," he told him, laughing. "I know I'm country, you city motherfucker."

"Oh, you talking big shit, huh? Watch this city nigga burn your ass at that rim, too," he shot back. They got into an easy, talking shit match that felt comfortable. He did it mostly with Blooney and Kevin, glad he and his roommate had that kind of energy so fast.

He low key thanked Mercedes for influencing his parents' decision to let me accept Duke's offer to leave Miami. Truthfully, he wanted a break from being affiliated with his family back home. They were well-respected, even feared but he got tired of hearing "Ain't you Keyz's son?" or "Hey, Chico's boy. Where your daddy at now?"

By then, even though the hood knew the story, both men had so much clout, people knew not to speak on it short of asking him who he was. Here in Durham, he was his own man. His own person.

By the time they hit the walkway that led to the cafeteria, Ishmael heard his stomach growl. The smell of fried chicken, mashed potatoes and other foods like cornbread, candied yams and stringed beans had him pick up his pace, his mouth watering and all.

"Got damn, Ice," Reno teased, hitting his gut that was firm that only made his start to growl next.

"Yeah, what was that you were just saying now?" Ishmael shot back, as he chuckled.

"I know! This bitch said 'feed me' and that's exactly what I planned to do. Smell good," Reno said, closing his eyes as he studied the aroma. "Let's go," he told Ishmael, damn near leaving him.

Once inside, they saw the cafeteria was partially full but busy. Some were in the line, getting piles of food placed on the plate while others were already seated, waiting for drinks. It may have been called a cafeteria, but it was state of the art.

It could easily pass for a restaurant, staff moving around busily to wait on them hand and foot. They had everything to drink from carafes of cranberry juice, freshly brewed iced tea, lemonade, and an assortment of sodas.

Hitting the Purell pump, both swiftly rubbed their hands before they each grabbed not one, but two plates. While Reno talked up a storm, speaking to the women that were there to serve them, Ishmael studied his surroundings. He was a creature of habit, always taught to spot all exits whenever he entered a room. Nothing change, especially since he was out his comfort zone. Motherfuckers were getting shot on campuses, mad he didn't have his heat on him.

He didn't care what his fathers said, he was bringing it and did.

As the women eagerly spoke back, one girl caught his eye. Unlike the others, she gave a gentle nod, then smiled, but kept the chatter to a minimum as each athlete approached her with their plate.

Even still, she was personable enough, leaning forward just a tad to give each one her undivided attention if they had a question. She even shunned a few who threw a compliment her way, noticing she just smiled, before giving her attention to the next one in line.

When he got to her, he said nothing, waiting to see what she would do next. Her smile from this angle was even better, her cheekbones lifting that revealed the prettiest teeth with a slight gap in the front, her full lips enveloping them. They were not too big, but big enough as she softly tucked them before relaxing them as she waited for him to speak.

He was in no rush, taking in her eyes. They were brown, almost the color of her hot chocolate just like her skin. Ishmael noted they were soft and inviting, a little crinkle forming in the corners that made him smile. She looked young, but not too young as she wore a bit of confidence in full of a room of potential greats.

He liked that. She wasn't trying to get anyone's attention, but didn't shy away from them while there to do her job. From what he could tell, she had huge plaits underneath her hairnet. The kind Janet Jackson wore in the movie *Poetic Justice*.

That shit was hood but hot, a nice blue woven into the black. It was subtle, but enough to reveal she had personality, not giving a fuck what rich kids thought.

He liked that...too.

"Ice, the line," Reno whispered, nudging him lightly with his elbow.

He looked down at his plate that was barely full, knowing he couldn't be done. Especially since both of their stomachs were battling hunger. He had two rolls, coleslaw, and a few deviled eggs. That meant he was just getting started since they hot foods were up next.

"What's your name, ma?" Ishmael asked her, not paying Reno any mind.

She frowned just a little, wondering if she heard him correctly. "I'm sorry. Did you ask me my name or did you call me ma?" She was careful the way she spoke, hoping he wasn't some rich kid trying to fuck with her. She hated that "ma" shit with a passion. Sashay giggled but said nothing else as Ishmael eyed her down.

"Shut up," Pepper grunted under her breath, nudging her. Ishmael saw the exchange, grinning as her friend got a kick out of his introduction.

Where he came from, a female was shorty, baby girl, ma, bae or worse—bitch, but only when she really was a man's bitch as in his girl. He figured Durham got down like that too, watching the black beauty before him slightly cut her eyes at her friend.

"Answer him, *ma*," her friend said, then tucked her lips. She was cute too, caramel complexion with full lips herself. Both a tad bit on the hood side he could tell, but definitely eye candy.

Pepper, knowing she needed this job, quickly regrouped and cut him a smile... and he swore right then she took his breath away.

Cheeks full like a chipmunk, housing the prettiest smile that consisted of a gap between her teeth. The imperfection was perfect as she lightly pursed her lips, raising her eyebrows at him.

"I'm not interested in whatever this is you're seeking. You're hungry or nah?" she asked, giving him a taste of his own medicine. He seemed to be intrigued fucking with her, so she indulged but only a little.

"I am hungry…feed me," he said, making her world stand still as her eyes bucked.

"Damnnnn," she heard Sashay say lowly, staring at Ishmael then back at her friend.

His father told him eyes never lied, but shorty was lying right now. She enjoyed the little interaction they had, her voice caught in her throat as she tried to process what happened. He knew what happened.

She met Ishmael, the motherfucking Iceman and he wanted her… bad. He didn't know why, but shorty had rearranged his attitude just that fast as he went in for a second round.

"Excuse, Miss. My bad. That was rude as shit. What's your name?" The line was growing long, a few of the guys leaning forward then back to see what the hold up was. Most said nothing while a couple sucked their teeth, mumbling under their breath.

"Well, it's not ma," she said, a smirk slightly forming that turned into a smile

"Word?" he said with a drawl that made her center jumped.

Wow, she thought to herself, clearing her throat. She knew like most of them he wasn't from around the way, his accent screaming he was from the south. She figured Atlanta at first, noting all the tattoos that decorated his forearms and biceps, but caught the diamond fronts he wore at the bottom. That alone told her was from Miami.

"Word, and it's Pepper."

"As in salt?" he laughed, hoping she eased up just a little bit.

"No, just Pepper."

"And I'm Sashay," her friend chimed in, happy to see her girl hadn't ran him off.

"Bro, what's up?" Reno asked, hearing the rumbling as they held up the line.

"I like that," he said, ignoring his roommate.

"So, what can I get you?" Pepper asked, dropping her head to hide her smile.

"You don't want to know my name?" he asked, pulling every bit of that smile out of her as she lifted her head.

"Not really, but go for it. The line's backed up and they seem... hungry like you," she said, noticing a few of the girls in the back that worked with her murmuring too. She had no desire to fuck with any of these athletes but many did, glancing over her shoulder as she dared them to say something.

When they didn't, she gave him her full attention. This time with no smile as she was ready for him to move on. She had responsibilities at home and being a side chick to him or anyone else wasn't something she was interested in.

"I would say fuck that line, so I will," he chuckled, then said, "Fuck that line."

"Yoooo," one teammate he assumed called out followed by a gang of responses that he drowned out.

"Yeah, but it's Iceman."

"Pleasure to meet you, Iceman." She didn't like he tossed her a name his mother clearly didn't name him, but it didn't matter. She didn't plan to speak to him on a personal level anyway. Catching her attitude, he grinned.

"Well, Iceman on the court, but my mother named me Ishmael. Ishmael Payne."

"Say, we not in an interview," another one called out as the others began to laugh. "Dude trying to apply for a job. I thought he came here to play ball. Not cook and serve!" While the dude who chose to clown him really started to get under his skin, Ishmael stood firmly, not budging at all.

"Uh, we better—" she said, watching her manager step out from the back.

"Fuck her, too," he said, winking his eyes. He could tell her boss, manager or whoever she was wasn't feeling shorty, making him stand there even longer.

Whew. He's so fine...and arrogant, she thought to herself but snapped out of it as her manager approached her from behind.

"Pepper, " she said, just above a whisper. "Are we good over here? Sir, is she giving you a problem?" He noticed the older woman had stained teeth, possibly from drinking coffee.

Her tinted her was a light purple and she had a mole on the side of her nose the size of a raisin. Her dark skin was dry and her gel had dried up around the edges underneath her cap.

"Oh, yes. He's uh, kinda slow," she said, easing in a slight diss he caught that only amped him up but knocked her on her ass.

"She's right. I'm slow, but some things are worth the wait. Nah'mean?" he said, his left brow lifted just a tad bit as he slid in a New York accent. Pepper almost melted, unsure of what to say next.

Who are you? she asked herself, losing this tango they had going on terribly. She was sure she was blushing now, feeling warm as Sashay playfully fanned her.

"Girl, I know that's right."

"Well, make it quick. And you," she said, leaning Pepper's ear. "Come to the back when the line is done."

"Yes, ma'am," she said, clearing her throat when the same guy yelled out, "Yo, boss man! No fraternizing with the help. Got damn, homey."

Ishmael's head quickly shot to the left as he slowly released his tray. Where he came from, that was straight disrespect. He gave no fucks she was working a minimum wage job. Plenty athletes that are millionaires were raised by mothers doing the same job as Pepper. And she was a woman. That was two strikes as his mouth was working on a third one, getting the crowd all worked up.

"Bitch nigga, what you said? Who the fuck you think you're talking to?" he fumed, as Reno held his forearm.

"Hey, Ice. Chill, man. Fuck him. He's whack for real."

"Hell, fuck naw," he told him, snatching away. In no time, Ishmael was on the dude's ass, gripping my his throat. With fingers as long that stretched as wide as his, the dude could barely breathe.

He was easily three hundred pounds, but was shorter and stouter, looking around anxiously for someone to intervene.

"Apologize to the young lady," Ishmael snarled, his voice low and steady.

He was ready to beat dude's ass if he didn't in the next three seconds, fully prepared to catch that flight. Then have his truck shipped back home. He had a mother he loved dearly, an aunt and baby sisters he'd die for before he allowed anyone to disrespect them. And that now included Pepper, whether he knew her or not.

He could tell Pepper didn't even know how bad she was, quickly taking in her small frame underneath the cafeteria smock. There sat two nice round C cups that complemented her hips that held up, he assumed, a nice size ass. She couldn't be no taller than 5'2", 5'3" at the most, gauging how her neck extended to look in his eyes before this battle ensued.

Yes, just that quickly, he peeped all of that but, anger burying his good time with her when he heard old boy trying his gangster.

"Who the fuck you supposed to be?" the guy managed to say, once Ishmael let him loose, pushing him in the chest with both hands.

"Ask your fucking neck, *fuck boy.*"

"I'm the fuck boy, but it's you—" he said before Ishmael punched him dead in his mouth.

A gang of "ohhhs" and "ahhhs" could be heard when Reno tackled him from behind pulling him back. "Ice dude, come on now. They probably about to call coach."

The guy laughed, wiping his mouth as blood leaked from the side. "You hit like a bitch."

"You felt like a bitch, *bitch.* Wearing a motherfucking training bra."

"That's enough!" the cafeteria manager called out. "It's the first day. We got all year to fight and on the court. Now, I will pretend this didn't happen if you two can shake it off," she said, grinning as she looked the two young boys up and down.

Over the years she had her a few to play around with, low key upset that Pepper had snagged Ishmael's attention so fast. She knew she would, upset they even hired her. Payne. Her grandkids loved Ishmael and she wanted to love on him if she got her shot. Now, she couldn't if Pepper had her paws him day one. At forty-two, she still was pulling them in and Ishmael was the right size, height and all. It was called having no teeth. That alone seemed to work in her favor.

Immediately, he felt a soft hand on his, causing him to look down. It was Pepper. Her eyes were no longer smiling, neither was she. She was concerned, gently wrapping what part of his hand she could hold on to as she silently urged him to come with her.

She wasn't strong enough to loosen his tightly clenched fist, but she hoped her presence alone could make him rethink his steps. She was used to the insults, heard them all the time when she ignored most dudes on the street.

That last thing she cared about was what some rich kid said about her. That was to be expected and since none of them cut her a check, she could careless what he said.

"It's okay. Trust me, it is," she spoke softly, her thumb grazing the back of his hand a few times to get him to release his fist and grab her hand.

"It's okay for this muhfucka to disrespect you?" he asked, lifting his right brow. Pepper knew it wasn't, but to diffuse the situation as quickly as possible, she hoped her next move would work.

"That muhfucka, as you would call him, is a fucking nobody *to me*. What he says don't matter. He doesn't know me, but he wants to," she said, shooting the dude a menacing look. "Ain't that right?" she asked they guy, lifting her right brow too.

He'd been licking his lips the entire time she stood there before he gripped his dick.

"Don't ask him that shit," Ishmael told her, his eyes never leaving the dude's. "And it does. Now apologize."

"Bro, I don't even know you, but come on now. Just apologize to the young lady before Ice spazzes out for real," Reno said, a slight chuckle following. "Motherfucker got hands big as fuck. Got damn," he said more to himself, shaking his head.

"Sorry," he mumbled.

"Fuck no. It's sorry, Pep—"

"No, it's okay," she stopped Ishmael, this time slipping her fingers through his. He looked down, liking the feel of them and the contrast of her chocolate skin against his.

"A'ight," was all Ishmael said, then shot her smile.

"Thank God," Pepper sighed, strengthening her hold on his hand. "Let's go."

Not waiting for consent, she tugged on his hand, leading him back to the line. Pepper didn't know who this man really was but one thing was for sure, he had her and every single woman's panties wet in there as he introduced himself hood style to the entire basketball team at Duke University.

The Iceman was there.

"Here," she said, handing him his plate once she got around on the other side. "Now, let me finish my job...and thank you."

"For what?"

"Just thank you," she said, looking at her manager. He caught the silent plea in her eyes for him to cooperate, too. He liked them a lot. Deciding to let it go, he sighed and shot ole boy a look who didn't say a word.

"A'ight, cool. It's your world...ma," he said and smiled to get her to smile back. Then rattled off a few things he saw so he could get out of her way.

He wasn't cool with how things played out, still fuming as he wanted to drop his tray and kicked dude to sleep. He didn't even know Pepper like that. Had no intentions on even stepping to a female, but somehow he had and she was stuck with him.

He didn't care what she said. No dude on the team was talking to her short of ordering food as he looked around, glaring at them.

"Yo, Ice. You wild," Reno told him, biting into his pork chop sandwich he made himself as they both sat at ate.

As he did, he studied her like an exam as she went back to work. How she moved, how she walked, how she interacted with the other athletes, offering napkins and wiping down tables. All the while, she hadn't missed a beat, paying him no mind.

He appreciated that even more. That meant him being who he was, was nothing to her. She didn't care he came from Miami, winning three high school state championships with seven offers all over the country. She didn't care he was in the blogs or even knew that he was. She curved him the same way he assumed she would curve the average dude, turning him the fuck on.

Before he left, he made one last trip by the table where the dude sat quietly, his eyes avoiding Ishmael as he approached the table.

"Every time I see you, I'ma fuck with you because I can. Make you fucking miserable. You'll think twice about minding my business and being a fuck boy. You wanted to holler at her, then do that shit. Don't be a pussy, *pussy*," he warned him lowly, patting him on his back before he walked off.

"I guess this is it, huh? All year round," Reno said and laughed, watching the guy nod his head quickly. "Big ass is scared."

"He should be," he replied, walking out of the cafeteria.

Pepper's eyes followed him, wiping the table down hard as she did. She fought hard to pretend to ignore him, exhaling once she saw the door finally close.

"Shining the table or cleaning up?" Sashay teased from behind, catching her off guard.

"Girl, shut up," she said and smiled, jumping just a little. "Don't do that."

"No, you don't pretend you wasn't feeling his fine ass. And remember, don't say shit to Ms. Harris. That bitch got it in for the both of us."

"Whatever. Since when did you start paying attention to who's who and giving dating advice?"

"Since I decided Fat Fat need a new uncle and maybe daddy. Hell, whichever come first. Just go," she told her, taking the towel and small bucket of water from her.

As Pepper took that walk, nothing could make her forget how he made her feel. Somehow Ishmael reminded her that there were still real men around out there. Real men who clearly had been raised right. That alone made her pick up her pace so she could get back to work. She knew they could never be anything, but she wasn't opposed to serving him personally all school year old to pretend that they were.

Besides, girls like her never got guys like him. She figured that didn't exclude her from daydreaming about him though.

CHAPTER 8

"*H*ey, shawty," one dude called out to Pepper as she walked to the bus stop. It was eleven o'clock at night. Her feet were killing her and she had a slight headache. She picked up that second shift, trying to make some extra money for the holidays while Sashay took off.

She had a little girl and a deadbeat baby daddy. He pretended to be a live-in nanny who called her promptly at three o'clock to make sure she was headed straight home. Pepper couldn't wait for her girl to get rid of him but said nothing since growing up in a two parent household was rare these days. Even if it was Sashay was providing financially for all three of them.

She was the mother and father at home, wanting to do everything possible to hold it down as much as she can. Especially since Drew and Bryce worked hard over the summer attending summer school. So anyway she could motivate them to keep it up by giving them an allowance and money for school to get a snack, she did.

Carrie had proved she wasn't shit, not even getting them school clothes for the new school year let alone an allowance or even filling out their free lunch application. Pepper had been forging Carrie's signature since fifth grade that she sometimes signed her mother's name on her own checks.

When it was time to purchase school uniforms, which was all on Pepper too. But with the help of Sashay, she had the uniform voucher hook up. Her aunt ran that program, sliding her an third voucher since the boys were so rough on clothes.

With the summer job she had at KFC after graduating, she managed to save up five hundred dollars. It wasn't much after working almost three months, but the food was free at the end of the night. So it was a win/win to take home.

That cash went fast too, grabbing them both the latest Jordans, of course hot, compliments of Sashay too, along with a book bag, under-clothes, and a coat for the wintertime. Nothing too expensive, but something just enough to keep them from catching a cold and hair-cuts. The school supplies came from the local church. They invited all of the locals out to pray over their children for the new school year.

She was a true hustler, scared to death sometimes she wouldn't make it but always found a way. It was that same hustle that linked her up wit Sasahy, a known booster whenever he wasn't working. And hooked up, becoming best friends when they both were arrested and went to juvie for a few months.

Pepper was sick, worried about Drew and Blake but God was faithful. They somehow made it work in spite of their mother Carrie, but Pepper had been beating herself up about it ever since. That was three years ago and she vowed never to do anything that could sepa-rate her from them again.

One night after going to bed hungry, she pulled out her cell and started looking for work. It had to be God when the Like page for Duke University came down her timeline. She had always wanted to go to college, but Duke was nowhere on her radar.

Now it was, quickly answering their "now hiring" ad online. With one click and less than a 15 percent charge on her cell, Pepper zipped right on though that online application. She had 2 percent left by the time she was done, but that was used checking her email for confir-mation to make sure it went through.

Once hired, she had one hundred and fifty dollars left after taking care of the boys. With that, she took twenty-five dollars to buy a pair of blue pants, fifteen for a white polo uniform top for work and twenty-five for to get a proper bra. One that could support her large breasts given her size.

With the eighty-five dollars she had left, she used coupons from her JCPenney's app to order herself two pairs of Converse with their buy one get one half off deal. That left her with forty-five bucks. She took to that to get her a monthly bus pass with fifteen dollars left over.

Pepper was resourceful, but it didn't hurt that she was a stunning, chocolate beauty who stayed to herself and minded her business. She was well liked in the neighborhood by most, even if Carrie wasn't. The OGs would slide her brothers a few dollars to keep them off the street from hustling, while she politely turned it down.

She didn't want a hand out. She wanted stability with no strings attached and that came from the money she made herself, then managed it as best as she could until the next check came. Pepper knew how to use milk and turn two eggs to four, used the ends of a loaf of bread to make French toast and lemonade with a splash of concentrated lemon juice with sugar.

"Aww, baby girl! Don't do me like that, shorty!" the guy yelled out his window as he drove slowly next to her. When she got to the bus stop, she took a seat and started scrolling through IG.

She wasn't with the shits now, shaking her head. She was tired of the cat calling peppered with pet names that didn't bare a resemblance to what her mother named her. Her patience grew even short when she heard the car door closed.

"Fuck," she grumbled, hoping he took this L respectfully. She heard him clap, then rub his hands as he approached her, knowing she couldn't just run off.

He saw those thunder thighs from way up the street, slightly bowed carrying a boat load of ass. Even under the coat she wore that struggled to stay underneath. She'd outgrown it two years earlier, but it was all she had for now, so she made it work.

"Baby girl, why you acting like you didn't hear me?" he asked her, licking his lips. He imagined sucking on her pussy, because from the looks of it, he knew it would be sweet.

He didn't look to be that much older than her, teeth iced out as he left his Mercedes Benz running. Pepper knew his kind. He was a dope boy who had a different girl for every day of the week. On his wrist was an even more expensive Rolex than the one Ishmael wore plus a thick, roped bracelet on the other. Three chains on his neck made him look like a fool. A rich one, but a fool that wasn't used to money, wearing it on his body and in his mouth instead of investing it.

His outfit alone probably was more than two month's pay, which screamed attention seeker as he wore every label starting from his fitted to his shoes. She hated attention, avoided it as much as she could but clearly ole boy was not there with her. So, no matter how long he stood there pleading his case, as long as he didn't touch her, Pepper was good.

"Oh, I see how you moving, baby girl."

"My name's not baby girl," she said, fighting hard to keep her cool as she applied a fake smile on her face. This day was already long and complicated with the stunt Ishmael pulled earlier and now this. "And thanks for I guess speaking, but I'm good."

"You sure?" he asked then took a stroll down her body. He noticed the coat missing buttons with a few food stains on her pants from work. She knew dope money when she saw, eyeing him back as he wore a Ferragamo leather coat, a chocolate and tan turtle neck and chocolate jeans. He was slim, hair faded and lightly waved with a goatee. His tan complexion accentuated his gold teeth as he broke out in a big smile. Too bad, however, it was short lived once they were interrupted.

"Pepper," they both heard, looking quickly behind her unwanted guest.

Damn, it's him...again, she thought, her mouth slightly agape as he walked up, damn near in between the two of them.

"Hey," she said softly, the air thinning out strangely as he approached them.

"Baby G—I mean, Miss Lady, this you?"

Pepper was about to tell him "no", but couldn't Ishmael answered for her instead.

"You see me, don't you?" Ishmael asked him, easing up in his face.

"I do," he replied and smirked, looking him up and down.

"Then why the fuck you asking her then?" He then shot Pepper a look, daring her to say otherwise as she slightly rolled her eyes. She was over the entire day and their male egos.

"Sloan," the dude said then grinned once he recognized Ishmael.

Durham was smaller than Miami, but not that small, that people didn't know him. He'd been all over ESPN for the past three years and all the city talked about once he decided to come attend Duke. "Congrats on your school ride, Ice. Sorry 'bout that, but when I saw her walking, I figured she was...single."

"Naw, just hardheaded," he told him, still looking at Pepper. "Imagine my woman walking around out here like her dude is straight slumming, got her on a bus stop."

"Women," Sloan said, this time curling his lip up at her with disgust. "Handle that. And again, congrats, homey," he said directly to Ishmael, now not even looking at her. When he hopped in his car and pulled off, Pepper soon realized why they called him Ice.

"Ayyye!" she squealed, when he scooped down and picked her up. No smile at all, growling lowly when he felt her soft body against his. In that moment, he wanted to drape all her thick ass and thighs in a blanket, knowing exactly why old boy stopped.

She'd been running around in his head since earlier, forcing him out of his room to get his mind off of her. He never once thought he'd run into her this time of night and on the bus stop.

"Please, put me down," she managed to say, squirming as he held on to her tightly.

"Why?"

"Why what?"

"Why should I put you down? You out here looking to be picked up, so I picked your ass up," he said with attitude. His knitted brows and flared nose were evident he was mad, his voice rattling while low.

"Ugh," she fussed, crossing her arms or tried to. When she couldn't she stopped and dropped her arms, causing the to dangle. He could tell she was tired, feeling bad since he knew she'd probably been standing on her feet all day.

"Yeah, whatever," he mumbled, slowly lowering her down.

"Thank you very much!" she huffed. She stumbled just a little, but quickly recovered as she shot him a look. "You know that was so not called for."

"Neither is you sitting out here rapping to this nigger this time a night? You know what he wanted?"

"Actually I don't and it's called standing on a bus stop so I can go home. What is wrong with you people?" she spat, hating what he accused her up.

"I know what he wanted and I don't like it. Not one fucking bit," he growled, pressing his body against hers.

She squinted her eyes. A low growl escaped as she gathered her thoughts. She rolled her eyes, crossing her arms as she waited for him to reply. He was losing all his cool points, looking like a lame. The night was getting worse as the crisp air clearly fogged his brain up.

He was doing shit he would never do when it came to a woman and would lie on his mother if asked if he did. And while he tried to pretend it was only about her safety, it was more.

He wanted her, all of her, casting his eyes down at the same busted up coat that was missing buttons but saw nothing but beauty.

"He's gone now," she said just above a whisper, her voice abandoning her.

"And?"

"That means I'm safe. You can go now," she said, her voice louder now as she took a deep breath. His cologne, overpowering their space had her floating, wishing she was back in his arms. He wanted her to be too, touching the side of her cheek.

"I will when you get inside." He reached underneath her arm, pulling on the door handle to open it. Without asking for permission, he said, "Get inside, ma. It's cold as fuck out here and it's midnight"

"Pepper," she corrected him, almost leaning into his finger as she closed her eyes.

"That's what I said," he lied and smiled. "And open your eyes, Pep. I want you to see what I see when I look at you."

"And what is that?"

"A strong, beautiful black woman unsure if every man wants to fuck. I mean of course I do, but later for that. Just get inside." With that, he stepped back enough so she could move to the side. As he pulled it open, he motioned with his head for her to sit down.

"What if I said no?" she asked, then time sniffling. She knew her coat was too small and she had no hat.

"Don't make me show my ass again today. You like that, shorty," he told her, eyeing her as he heard her sniffling too. He eased up enough as she involuntary sat back, staring up at him.

He was tall, so tall that Pepper felt light-headed looking almost at the sky at him as he stood in the door. She sniffled again, eager for him to close it. When he didn't, she started to wonder if this was the right move. She couldn't afford to get sick and she needed sleep.

"Fucking cold," he grumbled, slowing closing the door. "Sit back, Pepper and strap up."

"What do you want from me?" she blurted out instead, hating he was all in her personal space. Even diagnosing her. She was like a fish out of water and he was in her town, her hood.

"To trust me," was all he said. She saw the sincerity in his eyes as wiped her nose with a crumbled up napkin she had in her pocket.

"Fine. I sort of left my hat."

"Just your hat?" he asked, seeing her neck exposed to.

"Well, that too," she lied.

"A'ight. Let me get you home. I'm about to freeze my mother-fucking ass off!" he laughed, closing the door. As he made his way around and got in, he looked over and liked what he saw.

She wasn't the richest female nor classiest one, but seeing her sitting up in his shit made him feel really good. She didn't come with all the bells and whistles the average chick from Miami came with in the hood, but she didn't have to. Whatever she had caught his attention, as he pulled off smoothly feeling like a million bucks.

After she gave him her address, the ride was quiet as each was stuck in their thoughts. Her processing the entire day, dreading the cold coming on while he was still tripping on how he'd been moving since their paths crossed.

"Hey, how about we just start over," she finally said, breaking the silence. She dabbed her nose and smiled, slightly embarrassed. "Hi, I'm Pepper. Pepper Murphy. And you are?"

He thought that was cute, wanting to pinch her nose as she wiggled it, but didn't.

"Ice."

She rolled her eyes and smiled, knowing it was not his real name. "Here we go again," she groaned followed by a laugh. "This is very interesting."

"I've heard that before about myself," he quipped, winking his ass.

"Asshole," she teased lowly, easing into a comfortable flow with him as he laughed.

"I heard that about myself too, but I'm also a pretty good guy I heard. My parents loved me, my siblings look up to me and shit, who doesn't know me and like me?"

"Are you serious right now?" She couldn't believe how inflated his ego was, yet was so laid back at the same time. They then moved on to what she did in her spare time, which was care for her brothers. He could tell she loved them the same way he loved his brothers and sisters. Outside of that, she told him very little but that alone told him enough.

She was guarded and had been hurt before—just like him. He had no clue what he was doing, but he was eager to know more as she pointed to her street.

"There on the left. Turn there," she told him a slight sigh escaping.

When he stopped and put his truck in park, Pepper immediately opened her door stepping out as she huffed with one foot on the ground. "Wait," he said all too fast, holding her hand. She looked down then up, close to shaking her head no but didn't. After he assaulted his teammate and almost a stranger, she was confident her just walking off now without incident was impossible.

"You sure?"

"Pep, move your ass," he told her, tucking his lips as he released her hand. "Come on."

"It's not too friendly out here."

"Well that's good then since I ain't friendly," he replied, grabbing his heat from underneath his seat. He slipped it in his joggers, pulling his jacket down. He was licensed to carry, wouldn't carry any other way. Keyz and Chico made sure of that even though his mother didn't know it.

"Oh my God," she grumbled, feeling anxious. "Really?"

"Pepper?" he said, motioning for her to end it as he got out and locked his door. "And wait," he told her until he made it next to her. He didn't give two fucks that she lived around there. She was with him now, immediately his responsibility.

. "Here," he told her, handing her a Duke skully she didn't even know he had grabbed from the back seat. His mother went crazy once they decided he was going, ordering up all kinds of paraphernalia. He remembered he left a few bags in the back on his ride to her house.

"Naw, I can't."

"Listen, we gotta work on this. It's called listening, then following my lead," he replied, standing there as the onlookers looked on.

He'd already peeped two to his right and one to his far left. If he had to pop one, the one on the right was getting hit first as a distraction. Then at least one of the two on his left. That alone would increase his chances of surviving if things got heated.

"Lower your voice," she cautioned him, knowing they would love to make an example out of him. He reeked money, something they didn't have. At least not regularly and legally.

"I'm good—better than good. I see them and they see me, but it's not what we see. It's what we feel," he said, patting his shit to let them know he had company.

He never looked for trouble, but he didn't run from it either. At home, he rarely had to make his presence known, but he could tell this Durham shit was going to require him to show he had more than court skills, looking slightly over his shoulder. When he did, one immediately recognized him.

"Aye yo, that's Ice," he heard one of them say.

"Word, for real?" he other another reply, as they all started talking over each other.

"Oh shit! That is him!" the third guy said.

Pepper couldn't believe how they all became star struck over a college boy, who wasn't so much of a college boy the way he was handling her right now. He was all man, all man on his boss shit.

"My mother raised a gentleman. So unless you a straight up hoe who don't respect herself, I will always be a gentleman whenever you're in my presence And if I see a need I can meet—" he said and paused, grabbing her hand. "—it's met."

Pepper's mouth was open, unsure what to say. This was foreign to her. She knew that would be short-lived once he stepped inside and if he saw Carrie. She had not tact and respect and her were like two bitches fighting that couldn't stand each other.

"But—"

"But nothing, girl and let me put this on," he said, taking initiative once more. He made it clear to her she didn't run shit in the short few hours since they met, standing there like a kid as she tugged the skully over her head. "Now, let's go."

As they walked up the walkway that led to the apartment building entrance, Ishmael could hear a rat piss but he knew he still had eyes on him. That's exactly what he wanted. As long as they kept their fucking mouth closed, he had no reason to show them his ass.

By now, Pepper suspected he was a live wire and he was. And up there in this new city, he had no one to contain that beast in him. No one to fight his battle and he preferred it the way too.

Walking up three flights of stairs was nothing to Ishmael but he could tell Pepper was beat. She looked like she was carrying the weight of the world on her shoulders, sighing as they approached her front door.

"Looks like this is it," she said, forcing a smile on her face.

"What time do you have to be to work tomorrow?" he asked, already planning the next time he would see her.

"Eight and I'm pulling another double."

"Word?"

"Yes, but you should get going. Those guys are there aren't security, " she teased, trying to get a rise out of him.

"They will need that shit before me, but let me see that," he said, referring to her cell phone.

"Look—"

Sighing, he just took it out her hand. "Unlock it, please."

He gave her a sly grin when she did, looking like a tall, butterscotch treat she wanted to eat. She fought hard not to stare in the truck, but she couldn't help it now. He was like there, all in her face and her space. Most guys didn't get past speaking, which was fine for Pepper after her bad experience with dating, but she refused to lie to herself.

Ishmael "Ice" Payne had piqued her interest. She punched in the password to unlock her cell, careful to not allow him to see. He then dialed his number and let it ring a few times until her voicemail came on.

Her voice was sweet in person but even sweeter when she left a quirky greeting.

"Cute... like you."

"Just cute?" she asked, playing right into his hand and boy did she wish she was in his hands. All parts of her body, dropping her eyes as she felt warm from excitement or illness. Either one, she was still in a happy place and it was all because of him.

Yeah, this one right here about to mine, he thought. He didn't see her struggle. At least not the way she did. He saw her hustle, her motivation, her need to protect herself while he just wanted to protect her. Then have to himself.

"The rest remains to be shown, not told, ma."

"There you go with them names," she laughed.

"Long as its me calling you them," he said, taking a step back so she could retire for the night. "Take care of that cold, too. Good night. If you need anything, holler."

"I won't and good night," she said before quietly closing the door. She pushed her back against it when it closed, silently screaming as she did her little happy dance.

Nothing in her life had changed that much, but then it did. She was happy, picking up her happy pace as she went to check in on the boys. Drew was snoring like always while Bryce as sleeping with his mouth wide open, drool dried up on the side of his mouth.

They were too cute. So cute, she snuck in a good night kiss. When she did, Drew mumbled something in his sleep while Blake grabbed her hand. Most nights, she struggled to fall off to sleep but not tonight. Tonight she had nothing but a Ishmael's cocky ass, yet soothing voice sounding off like a lullaby in her head.

CHAPTER 9

*B*right an early before sunrise, Ishmael was up, showered and ready to go. He already had his morning prayer with his mother, something he promised to do each day before he started anything. Sometimes it was with his aunt, but the day never caught him without prayer. Most times, he listened but he still remembered to say "amen". It was like sealing it with faith from his lips to God's ears.

When he stepped out, Reno was walking around, back all wet in his boxers and ear pods on. He was listening to a Meek Mills joint from what he could tell, mumbling a few words here and there.

"Ice!" he yelled loudly, both arms stretched out wide.

"Sup, boy," he told him, slapping his hand. He looked at his watch, ready to burn. They had less than an hour to walk to the cafeteria, eat and get to the locker room. They were told to dress for the weight room, prepared to spend at least the morning there.

"Not shit," he said, snatching one ear pod out. "I like to air dry," he said, walking to his room. "Bags still not here, but give me two minutes. I may have to buy some clothes today."

Ishmael already knew that would be a task given how big Reno was. It was hard shopping for him because of his height alone. Reno's mama was nothing like his because if Myriah found out his bag was anywhere but with him, she would have been there bright and early with bags on top of bags instead calling him to pray.

In less than two minutes, Reno surprisingly was dressed and ready to go. As they walked to grab a bite to eat, he told Ishmael about the kickback he went to the night before.

"Don't be fucking around smoking with these niggas, Ree. Remember, this right here is it. The key to our future. These muhfuckas will have you geeking on some laced bullshit," Ishmael told him, hoping his newfound friend was listening.

He wouldn't have to tell Blooney or Kevin that, but Reno was way too gun hoe for him to get in the mix so soon. The last thing he wanted to do was fuck up and prove his mother wrong. Besides, he smoked his own shit, reminding himself he needed to get him some from his Uncle Chello.

He had the best marijuana period if you asked him. He didn't smoke much, but if he did, he was smoking from his own folks. Chello, after twenty-years, still moved a lot of shit around, traveling all up down the east coast for his wife, Mulan.

That DEA movement was working in his favorite, but a reason he stayed in longer if he were being honest. Mulan loved her husband to a fault. On one hand, she wanted him out the game while the other, she kept him in there, giving him information to move product around without getting caught.

He chuckled. "Damn it, man," he said, thinking about Pepper. She could be his Mulan any day. She was dark like her too. Smart he detected, a tad bit sassy and a woman he knew wanted her own.

"Naw, they had just a few hookahs, beer and a few bottles. Cheap shit, but hey, we're in college. Besides, I ain't smoking shit I didn't buy and roll myself. You should have came, though. Dude was there. Shaking and all when I stepped in there."

"I'm straight and he should fucking shake, ole bitch boy. A straight broad. I'm here for the hoops, but his ass can get it. Understand?"

"You sure you don't know that fine ass chick from the café from before? You going hard, Ice," Reno asked him slyly, watching Ishmael's jaws tightened as he called her fine.

"New, I just hate when bitches talk down on people. My family didn't always have money and even though we got it now, that's their shit. Not mine. I'm up here trying to get my own bank account up. And what that fine shit, bro. I'll fuck you up too," he told him, then smiled but meant it when he said it.

His parents didn't think he knew the story about his mother being a hoe back in the day, but she was still his Queen. Hoe or not, she never once let him go without. That alone required his loyalty and respect, and so did Pepper.

"Don't let me find out you ready to body everybody behind her. And unlike that dude, I'll fuck you up...Miami," Reno said, smirking as Ishmael waved him off. "Y'all all think this country shit don't sting. Watch out, bro."

Ishmael was smiling hard like hell on the insides, eager to see her. as he ignored Reno. He didn't give a damn what he was talking about, walking faster as he continued to ramble on.

When they got inside, they immediately hit the sanitizer pump, then grabbed two plates to eat again. Ishmael was about to grab a third, wanting a reason to stand in front of her longer. He went down the line this time with his eyes down, wanting to sneak up on her.

As they passed an assortment of breakfast meat, Ishmael heard everyone's voice asking what he wanted except the one voice he wanted to hear. By the time he got to the end with his plate full of random shit, he just asked for. He then stopped and asked the last server, "Hey, Pepper's not here today?"

"Called out sick or something. Coffee, tea, juice, water?" she asked, looking at him like "now what".

"Yeah? And water," he said, wishing got her number yesterday.

"Okay. Next!" she yelled out, motioning for him to move. He saw Sashay smile weakly his way, but said nothing as he walked off with an attitude.

Just like that, he was in a fucked up mood again and it was all Pepper's fault.

Hell naw. You got to get it together, he thought to himself. *And fast.*

᪥

"*H*ere," Drew said, handing his lunch money back to Pepper.

"Boy, put that away," she fussed lowly, popping his hand. Carrie wasn't up and moving around, but she was listening. She always was.

"But you need medicine, sis," Blake said, offering his too.

"And I said put it away. I will be fine. Nothing one day of rest won't handle. Now zip those jackets up and grab your hats," she told them, preparing to walk them outside.

Her nose was so stuffy, her head was pounding, and she couldn't feel her face. She couldn't taste it either, drinking two cups of tea that didn't seem to help much. The hot water wasn't so hot to see if a hot shower would work. Then boiling water was more work for a hot bath that would grow cold by the time she stepped in it.

She had a few dollars. So with that, she planned to hit the corner store, hoping it was enough for some Nyquil. If not, honey and lemon juice would have to do while she rubbed her chest down with Icy Hot. She was going to sweat out whatever this was, already anxious about calling out.

It had only been a month, but Ms. Harris was definitely out to get her. When she called in, she wouldn't even come to the phone. That alone had Pepper spooked. She needed this job and bad, made with her own body for getting sick.

"Drew? Blake?" she called out to them, opening the front door. The brutal, crisp air hit her even in the hallway. Downing a sweatshirt over her head and then her coat, Pepper led them out and down the stairwell.

"You sure, Pepper?" Drew asked as they waited patiently for the bus.

"Hey," she said, grabbing him by the cheek as he smiled. "I'm going to be okay. You just remember what you practiced all weekend so you

98

can ace that math exam, okay bookie," she said, calling him by his baby nickname.

"Sis, for real?" he fussed softly, looking around as she grabbed one of his braids. The girls giggled, all thinking Drew and Blake were cute. Both with long braids and bushy eyebrows, they were pretty boys in the making. Even with their wide noses.

"What, you're not my bookie anymore?" she asked, poking her lip out.

Blake laughed, catching her attention. "Now why are you laughing, my baby bear?" He earned the named baby bear because he was so hairy as a baby. Drew was too, but Blake had twice the amount.

"Pep, mannnn," he fussed, but smiled, dropping his eyes.

"Awww, you know you like that," she cooed.

Both of them loved being loved on my Pepper. Carrie did have her soft moments when she wasn't drinking or just spazzing out, loving on them every now and again. But it was Pepper who made them understand the power of love. She didn't baby them, issuing tough love too from running off fast girls to putting them on punishment if they got a low grade on homework or a test.

Pepper was doing it all, but she would all day if she had to. Those boys were her life.

"Aye, yo Blake, the bus coming," Drew said, easing over to give Pepper a hug. "Sis, get some rest. And if I need to come home, just—"

"Just nothing. I'll be fine," she assured him, sniffling. "Now, go." When the bus pulled up, the kids tussled and pushed to get on while Drew and Blake lingered in the back. Pepper stayed right there, silently nudging them to get on. No matter how crappy she felt, she would stand in that cold air until they were securely on the bus.

Once it pulled out and rounded the corner, Pepper took off to the corner store when her cell rang.

"What's up, girl?"

"Bitch, why Ice came asking for you today?" Sashay belted all loud in her ear. Pepper could tell she had ducked off someone in the back, her voice muffled although booming. She froze when she heard that.

She wondered why, feeling butterflies flutter in her stomach for no reason at all if she were being honest. She didn't have time for him or no guy actually, yet felt her heart beating like a drum.

"Yeah?" she said, pretending to sound unbothered but squealing on the inside.

"Yes, girl. Then took off like he was mad. Anyway, I gotta go. Ethel's old ass on me today since you're not here. You know you're the most hated bitch, so now I'm getting it double. Hoe breath smell like garbage. Ass and garbage. The fuck wrong with her teeth?" Sashay said and giggled.

"Alpo!" they both said and laughed together. Alpo was her nickname from them because she looked like Scooby Doo.

"Oh, what happened? I tried calling you to see but your ass didn't answer. Then Fat Fat was up all night, blocking."

"Blocking what? You and Stevie fucking again?"

"Shit, he better. That's his pay for being there," Sashay said, snickering. "He can fuck. That's about it."

"Ugh, spare me. And anywhere, nothing really. Just how I need to seek assistance if they are giving me a hard time. Told me to watch what I wear like I'm the reason they acted like that. Bitch just mad because the dog pound don't want her and neither do these young ass boys with her gummy ass," Pepper told, causing Sashay to holler.

"Say that, horse smelling ass mouth," Sashay giggled. "Suck dick three times a day. She think we don't know about her? And you, my baby, sound like shit."

"I feel like shit, sis. But I'll be okay."

"You're good?" she probed, asking her about money.

"Yeah, it is what it is," she said and sighed. "Give Fat Fat a kiss for me," she said.

"I will. Bye, hoe."

"Says the hoe using her baby daddy for penis," she said and laughed before they hung up.

When she headed to the store, the scenery was the same. Nothing changed— the fiends were sleep and the trap boys were turning in after a long night. Short of a few "what's happening" and "hey" from neighbors speaking as she passed by, it was just she and her thoughts.

"Hey, Jody," she said, walking in as she headed to the isle that had a few medicine and household cleaning items. Looking around, most were item dusty, opened or old as she suspected. "Jody, when do you all plan to restock?' she yelled out, not looking up. When she backed up, she ran into someone who clearly knew her well, holding her close to them.

"Uh, excuse me," she said with an attitude, snatching away as she turned her head. "Bone? For real?"

"Aye, I was trying to get my aunt some bleach, Pepper. Put a blinker on that ass when you're backing up," he teased, eyeing her down.

Bone was older than Pepper—much older. When they were messing around, she was sixteen. He, however, was twenty-three. Pepper never had any intentions of dating anyone, but she fell victim early on to an absent, non-caring mother. As long as money was coming in the house, she didn't care what Pepper did and with Bone.

When they met though, he had a girlfriend. Her name was Tammy. She lived in the same apartment building on the first floor. Tammy was that bitch all the guys in the hood wanted to date, but Bone got her.

She was tall, thick, and very shapely. She earned her money at the strip club, never going to private rooms or having sex. Bone snatched her up early on being that he was the man the streets everyone watched as he came up. He wasn't moving the most weight but enough to get Tammy's attention and to call a few shots about who served around there.

When he did, he allowed her to keep working but took up a seat in the club to make sure there was no disrespect or fucking. And sat there he did like a faithful non-paying customer, day in and day out. Surprisingly, since she was that good, men came and spent money purely for the illusion, and while he was there.

That hustle nor love affair didn't last long when Bone caught a possession charge, one that had him down for three years with five on paper. As soon as he touched down, Tammy had moved on. He tried his hardest to get her back, but one thing's for sure—it doesn't take long for one man to step in where another man step off.

Within six months, she did more than strip. She ended up marrying the strip club owner, never once looking back for Bone. When he did touch down, the bitches he used to overlook for Tammy now overlooked him.

All except Pepper who'd been crushing on him since she was thirteen. So imagine at sixteen how wide open he had her once he came back? And it didn't hurt she had filled out, her body proportioned like a fucking porn star. It was all natural too.

Carrie welcomed him in right on in, never once acknowledging she was low key pimping out her daughter. All Bone saw was ass and pussy at first, but that young ass caught his heart.

Still, he felt the need to earn his street credibility back, being a hoe as he tried to impress bigger hoes. Hating Tammy made him forget about loving Pepper, getting caught more times then he cared to admit. Now, he was stuck.

He soon fucked around and had a baby with this girl named Kizzy. If cheating didn't do it, that baby did. Three years without her were three years too long for Bone. Still, he still found a way to be a friend, shooting her a few ends just to stay in her face. Well sometimes, since most times she rejected it.

So, anytime he saw Pepper, he put in time trying to find a way to get back into her good graces. He learned bullying didn't work. Not when she fought her own mother, so she didn't mind fucking him up with a bottle or the nearest thing she could find.

So he used money, the homey approach. Those two alone got him conversation, but boy, did he want more. He didn't even bother her daily like he used to, but one thing's for sure. He was not around. Just kept tabs from afar. She never once understood why guys didn't shoot their shot, but didn't give it much thought since dating wasn't a priority.

But many would tell you it was Bone. The streets knew he'd go goofy about her, so they fell all the way back.

"Yeah, okay," she said dryly, giving him her back.

"For real, Pep. She's been sick all week. My baby girl's there, so I got to go through that bitch and bleach it down. You sound sick, too."

"I'm straight," she replied, moving down the isle to get some lemon juice.

"I know you're straight, but for real, be careful. That can turn into something worse. Doctor said my auntie probably got bronchitis."

"Oh no, not Miss Laura," she said shockingly as she stopped and looked his way. Miss Laura was good people to Pepper. Her children weren't shit, especially Bone's father, Benjamin. He had at least six kids, all of them living at some point with Miss Laura. She kept a house full, even Bone which is how she used to see him.

"Yeah, but I got her. Right after I clean up, I'ma get her some soup and pick up her meds. Brielle already fussy, wanting to be held," he said, smiling when he spoke of his daughter. He didn't like her mother, but he loved his baby to no end.

"She's beautiful," Pepper said, thinking of how big she'd gotten. "I'm sorry to hear about Miss Laurie. Make sure you do what you said, too. She'd appreciate that."

"Tell her yourself," he slipped in, trying to get her to go back to the apartment with him.

"No, thank you. No longer my job," she shot back with a smile.

"It could be though, Pepper. But anyway, what about you?" he asked. "Would you appreciate it if I did something to help you?" he asked lowly, stepping in her space.

"Boy, your ass really trying today," she laughed and sniffled, wiping her nose. "And move before you get sick."

"I am sick. Sick in love."

"Ugh, begging doesn't look good on you. Especially when you dry begging, knowing you can't be faithful."

"Says who?" he asked her, closing the space between them. He admired Pepper's beauty all the more, wanting to kiss her lips. He didn't give a shit about a cold. Baby girl was bad to him, even dressed casually in some tights and a hoodie.

"We're good, Bone. No hard feelings, so let it go. I swear I'm over it. I've *been* over it. You got your baby and I got me."

"I do have my baby, but that don't have shit with what we could have, Pepper. Don't forget I wasn't always the bad buy," he said, coming in and putting his foot in quite a few men asses when Carrie started letting anybody come in there.

Grown men older than him didn't see a sixteen year old's ass. They saw a "grown woman's ass". He was twenty-three at the time his damn self, but he'd be damn if some old dude twice his age would fuck with his girl.

As he gazed down, he liked his lips. Pepper was still fine to him, rocking a pair of low top Converse to go with her outfit. She was still cute, braids pulled up in a ponytail. Her skin was smooth, she smelled good, too. "I know I fucked up."

"That you did," she said, tired of having this same, two-year-old conversation since he'd been out. "But things happen, Frederick," she said, calling him by his real name.

"Frederick? Oh, I see," he laughed. "Keeping it all formal and shit, but I respect that. I just want to right my wrongs, prove that I was childish as fuck back then. I'm on something else now. Got a warehouse job, stay out the streets.

When I'm not doing that, I check on my auntie and take care of my daughter. I couldn't tell you where her mammy is and honestly, I don't give a fuck. Next month, my baby will be in daycare anyway. Did the paperwork myself and all. Real shit, Pep," he said, walking with her as she grabbed some honey.

She was impressed, glad to see he finally stepped up. He still looked good himself, a nice goatee complementing his rugged cheekbones and pussy melting smell. Bones could have a bad day but he was no Ishmael. Just a dark, hood version.

"Well, the good thing is you learned from your mistakes. And I'm proud of you. Kids deserve a present parent," she said, thinking of Carrie and the absent father she knew nothing about. "It makes life easier for them."

Bone knew her story all too well, using it to capitalize off of it himself. He felt fucked up when she said that, another apology coming next when she stopped him.

"Look, I told you I forgive you. Besides, I was young anyway," she laughed, lightly touching his chest. "I had no reason to be fucking around with a grown man anyway. I was a kid. A virgin, right?" she said, shrugging one shoulder. "Nothing important. Who the hell cares about a being a virgin's first, then playing number two to every bitch that wants to fight her, right?"

Bone grimaced she politely unloaded on him, reminding him he was never getting her back. She had the memory and heartache to prove it.

"Damn, that was a fucked up way to say you forgive somebody," he shot back, then smiled. "But I deserve it, like I said."

By the time they reached the front counter, Bone slapped a twenty on there, paying for both of their stuff.

"Wait, that's my stuff," she said, grabbing his arm.

"It's still yours. And keep the change," he told her, grabbing the bottle of bleach off the counter.

"I don't need your money," she told him, waiting the cashier count out nine dollars.

"Pep, it's just nine bucks, my baby. I would give you more but you won't take my shit. So at least take that and get yourself your own soup."

"Hmmmm," she said to herself, feeling queasy from the headache and not eating.

"Pep, take it. And again, I'm sorry," he said, opening the door to head back on out to his aunt.

CHAPTER 10

"It doesn't matter what he feels like now, Mercedes. Men are like children. They want attention, they want to be worshipped, they want to feel like they are the only one."

"But he was, mama," Mercedes whined, still not being truthful about Petey.

Paris rolled her eyes and took a sip of wine. While most of the east coast was cold, she was still pretty around her pool sunbathing. She wouldn't trade sunny south for anything. Sure, she enjoyed skiing in Aspen or being on the mountains at a resort during wintertime, but Miami was it for her. Traveling and not footing the bill was one of the many benefits being with Big Wayne, even with Mercedes being grown now.

"If he was, then what changed, Mercedes?" she asked, thinking about her old crush Chico. She couldn't stand that damn Myriah, surprised he had actually gotten himself together.

He was a whole hoe, who barely looked her way after she had a few moments with him here and there when he was first coming up in the game. So, when she found out Myriah knocked down a boss of his caliber, she hated her even more. And now that her daughter couldn't snag his son, she was disgusted. "Just couldn't close the deal?"

"It wasn't a business proposition, mother," Mercedes huffed, donning her shades on her face to hid the mist in her eyes. "We were in a relationship."

All her life, she'd been poked and picked on by her mother. If it wasn't about her weight or skin complexion, it was about the guys she chose to date. Many she didn't find interesting, but if they had money or were attached to money, Mercedes was programmed to pursue them.

The madness started at twelve when she enrolled her in a gym with a personal trainer to lose weight. Then she had to train and develop muscle including enough to fill up her C cup bra size. From there it was skin peels after joining the cheerleading squad, the sun tanning her skin too dark for Paris's liking.

Big Wayne was as dark as they come, but his money was right and he was sexy as fuck. She prayed his complexion didn't become her daughter's and it didn't, but she still stayed on her.

"So you so," she mumbled, shaking her head at her daughter. She wanted to push her ass in the pool, but that would mean she'd get wet too. So she refrained.

"Mom, I'm not like you," she said softly, hating the front she'd been putting on all these years.

"What the hell is that supposed to mean, little girl?' she snarled, sitting up quickly. "You are like me. What, you think I put in all this work for you to be less than me? Fuck no. I told you from before he wasn't shit, but noooo, you just had to prove me wrong.

Now, look at you sitting over there with your puppy dog eyes, married to that cell and social media. He doesn't give a fuck about you. Check the blogs, the posts and all. He's a hoe. Clearly, that boy ain't thinking about you," she laughed, tossing her hand at her like "chile please."

"Really, Paris?" Big Wayne said with authority, walking outside. Mercedes sucked her teeth. Sure, she was checking for Ishmael because she hate she had hurt him. She did want to love him, but someone else was in the way. Someone she knew Paris wouldn't approve of—Petey.

Now she felt like nothing, Big Wayne disgusted with himself as he caught Paris on her bullshit. He wanted to tell his wife that Mercedes was years ahead of her in class and morals, but before he disrespected the way he wanted to, he had to see about his child first.

"Wayne, don't start," she said, holding up her hand. "I'm just telling her what we both know. That boy played my baby. He is just like his parents. Especially that trash of a mother and you know it," she said, waiting for him to defend Myriah.

Like Paris had her fling with Chico, Big Wayne dibbled and dabbled with Myriah. Nothing serious, but she managed to dig her claws into his pockets back in the day. She was cool too, and very easy going whenever Big Wayne pulled up to a local spot where the girls hung out at.

And don't let it be a chicken wing spot. He'd show out, buying food and drinks for everyone while he sat in his box like Chevy that sat low playing from the infamous Miami group, Uncle Luke and the 2 Live Crew. Even tossed them a few dollars just to "show love" as he'd put it, Myriah being one of them.

He was over it, but clearly his wife was not and he hated it. It was tearing his daughter up, who at eighteen, could leave home now and never speak to them. To this day, Big Wayne would never confirm nor deny it if he actually slept with Myriah, but Paris knew it.

He'd shown Myriah love on more than one occasion, when out and out on the streets over the years, but still she had no proof. So, when Mercedes brought Chico's eldest, Ishmael home, it was like payback to shut Paris up. That is until Mercedes messed it up.

"I don't know anything and neither do you. Paris, it's been like twenty years. Our kids are adults now. Grow the fuck up," he told her, reaching for his baby girl. "Come here."

Mercedes reached under her shades, dabbing her eyes with the back of her hand before she shook her head no. She knew Paris. Any sign of her siding with Big Wayne would be trouble for her later on.

Paris wasn't a physically abusive mother, but she learned how to beat her down emotionally, reminding her that it was her hustle, putting up with Big Wayne and all his bitches that got her the life she was living now.

"No, daddy. I'm okay."

"No, you're not. Besides, I need you to take a ride with me. I want to show you something," he said, still waiting for her to grab his hand. When she did, he pulled her up and smiled. "You know you're still the best thing that's ever happened to me, right?"

"Yes, daddy," she sniffled. He managed to get a smile out of her as he pulled her in for a hug.

"Good. And any motherfucker that ain't fucking with you is the loser. Never you, baby girl. Never you. Now go ahead inside, wash your face, and meet me out front in a few. Okay?" he asked, leaning back as he gazed at his beautiful daughter.

Just like that, Mercedes felt lighter. She was still sad, wanting to tell her daddy everything. She almost would have, but felt her mother intense stare, lightly gritting her teeth.

"Yes, daddy. I won't be long," she said, hugging him once more.

"Make sure you put something under those eyes, Mercedes," Paris just had to slip in. "You look like you've aged, all that crying."

"Yes, ma'am."

Once she was out hearing distance, Big Wayne went in.

"So, you think your pussy that good that I got to stand around and let you fuck with my daughter, P?"

"Oh God, he here goes," she mumbled, settling into her chair after she lowered it just a little more, then she closed her eyes.

"Yeah, hear I go. My baby is eighteen, bitch. I don't owe you shit. Never did. I had a gang of hoes that would have easily come in and nursed your baby with their own motherfucking titty milk. Shit, yours too. But I respected you didn't kill my seed, giving me a reason to get my shit cleaned up.

Understand though, my baby, if I have to, it's still not too late. Now, whenever we get back, clean that shit up. Apologize to my baby girl and stop acting like a fucking baby yourself, Paris.

Niggas not hard up for pussy when bitches giving it away and I never was. You caught me slipping when I slid into that average pussy and busted one," he snarled lowly, carefully looking at the door that led into the house.

"If my memory serves me correctly, this average pussy has kept you all these years. No baby makes a man stick around. You could have been a first a month daddy," she said with a slight grin on her face, lifting her left eyelid to watch him fume.

"I could have but I wanted to be the number one man in her life. You don't know anything about that, though."

"You're right, I don't," she said, her voice laced with venom. "Can't even be loyal to a motherfucker that openly shows disdain for his wife and get respect."

"Oh, I respect you, but see, that's where you're wrong. The disdain comes from motherfuckers knowing you just wanted a piece of what came with me and you got that. Look around," he said, his hand waving at the lavish house they lived in. "You don't want respect, Paris. You've always wanted power, still do. Shit, you don't even want love because if you did, you'd love that little girl in there fighting so hard to get you to love her back."

Paris' head shot up, looking his way. She couldn't believe he was calling her out for being emotionally available when he'd been that with her the entire time they'd been together.

"Yes, baby. She loves you and, if I'm being honest, I love you too. I just don't like you," he told her, dragging his hand down his mouth before he smiled. "Be ready to apologize when we get back. Cook dinner. Send April home tonight and be a wife and mother, P. I kinda got used to that average pussy," he said slickly, winking his eye. "Later, baby."

As Big Wayne took a slow stroll past her, looking finer than he did even twenty years earlier, Paris did everything she could not to curse him the fuck out. She couldn't understand why he was so hard on her being cold and callous when she learned it from him.

"Oh, salmon, asparagus and garlic mashed potatoes," he told her, turning around. "That's Mercedes favorite meal, but make me want a rib eye. Can you handle that?" he asked her, lifting his right brow.

"Sure, Wayne," she said, a fake smile plastered.

"Good. See you later, Paris. And remember, a nigger love you. I know I show it in a fucked up way, but maybe one of us can start trying to be the bigger person. Maybe that's me... or you."

"Yeah, Wayne. Maybe that is me," she said, turning her legs to the side as she stood up. Big Wayne still thought Paris was fine as fuck, her tanned, thick thighs holding all that ass up nicely. But he wanted more than an arm piece now. He wanted love, respect, and peace for all of them.

ॐ

"So, talk to me, baby. What's going on?" Big Wayne asked Mercedes, watching her stare out the window. She was extremely quiet, every now and then staring at her cell.

"Life, daddy," she said, taking a deep breath before she looked his way. He was all smiles, loving his daughter to no end. She was all him, physically and emotionally, loving others sometimes to a fault.

"Baby girl, you're just getting started," he laughed, shaking his head. "What's up with life that has you so down? You have a full ride to a pretty decent school, money, clothes, you're healthy, smart. Shit, way smarter than me," he had to add, wondering what life would be like if Paris weren't her mother.

"So you say, daddy but thank you." She gave him a forced smiled, then looking at the trees that were now in a blur the deeper they got into the secluded yet exclusive area called Coral Gables. "So, where are we going? A new business venture," she asked, squinting her eyes.

She loved to see her daddy hustle, coming up with new ideas and ways to make money. Sure she loved he was respected in the streets and his name alone had influence, but he had great work ethics and was fair for the most part.

He employed quite a few people from the hood, numbers growing each and every time he thought of what else he could do to never be broke. He remembered those days, wishing he didn't have to steal shit or eat out the garbage can.

As soon as he could make a few dollars, hustling on the corner, he knew he would be a boss. While most took their money, trying to look the part, Big Wayne took his earnings and re-upped slowly. He didn't care about the latest anything, slowly building his own team.

Life was good, eager to be a black Scarface himself and was on some level until God decided to bless him and make him a daddy. Mercedes had saved his life. So, before he allowed Paris to fuck it up, he was doing something about it.

"Have I failed you, baby?' he asked Mercedes instead, praying she would say no.

"Failed me how, daddy?" she asked, sitting up as she looked at him.

"Shit," he said and shrugged. "Coming up short, not being there. Making you feel like you couldn't be yourself or talk to me."

Mercedes immediately thought of Petey, remembering all the nights they talked until the moon rose followed by the sun. Petey was one of the good ones, never wanting to disrespect his boss. He even stepped down from hustling hard when Big Wayne took a personal interest in him.

He always told Mercedes, *"You're the only one that could make me fuck up with Big Wayne, baby. And I mean that."* Still, he never did. Even though Paris thought she could be happy with Ishmael, it was Petey that held all the cards. She only chased him to clear her name, the blogs killing her image.

She had big dreams, her clothing line and college. And she did love him on some level. She just wanted to fess up finally and tell the whole truth, but ego and pride were motherfuckers. So she started showing out on social media instead.

"Of course not, daddy. I'm the luckiest girl in the world. I mean how many of my friends have a daddy so fine like he still a jit?" she said, using his term "jit" as in being young.

"Look at you talking about me looking like a jit. What you know 'bout that word?" he asked her, pulling in front of an empty building, no cars in the parking lot except one. And one she didn't recognize as she shot him a look.

"Daddy, uh where are we?"

"Answer me, and stop skating around my question, Mercedes," he chuckled.

"Daddy, you know you and mommy be playing ole school music, singing and um…" she stopped and laughed. "Anyway, I know. That's all you need to know," she shot back with the cutest smirk on her face.

"Yeah, yeah," Big Wayne said. "And I'm not blind, baby. Absent sometimes, but not blind. This right there is me investing in your future. The world is yours, Mercedes. It's all yours."

"Petey says it all the time," she squinted and smiled, dropping her eyes. Big Wayne caught that, nodding his head.

"Oh, he does, does he?""

"Yeah, daddy. He got an old soul hanging out with you," she said with a light chuckle.

"So that's it. You calling me old but not Petey, baby girl. I'm starting to them he got a thing for you or you for him," he teased, pulling her over as he hissed her forehead.

"Daddy!" she squealed, then jumped when someone tapped on his window. "Oh shoot! He scared me." It was Petey, standing like a boss with his hands in his pocket. When Big Wayne rolled the window down, he shot him a nod.

"Sup, Big Wayne? Mercedes?" Petey said, subtly clinching his jaw.

"Nothing much. You got that?' he asked him, releasing Mercedes as he hit the locks on the door.

"Yes, sir," he said, dangling the keys up for him to see.

"Alright. Baby girl, come on. Let's go."

"Are you serious? What's really?" she said, her legs shaky as she stepped outside his truck to stand. Petey's eyes boring into her made her uneasy, yet her heart skipped a beat or two as she caught her breath.

"Your studio…fashion studio," Big Wayne said with a wink, watching her as a faint smile began to form.

"Daddy?" she said softly as she gasped.

"Come on, spunk," he said, waving her over.

"Daddy?' Mercedes said again, this time her eyes watery.

Petey felt his heart swell, wishing it were him that could have done it for her. Still, he smiled and nodded at Big Wayne as they got out and approached the building. It was not too big but big enough.

Chic and edgy at the same time as the furniture was hot pink and gold, her favorite colors. The entire room had that art deco look with black and gold manikins around for sizing.

"Petey, go and show her around," Big Wayne said, watching her shake as she stood there.

As he eased his hand out slowly, Mercedes looked down at it but when she looked up and her eyes met Petey's. She pursed her lips, feeling butterflies in her stomach. It was as if they were alone, Petey's brown warm eyes sucking her in. He loved Mercedes almost half of her life.

He wanted to tell Big Wayne this was his responsibility, still looking for ways to get his money up for her. Mercedes may have enjoyed the finer things in life, but when she was with Petey, he saw a different side.

She was a brat, but when it was just the two of them, Mercedes sat around googly-eyed, talking about her dreams. Sure she was a bad ass chick would could have the best of them, but she wanted him. He just refused to live in the shadow of her father no matter how good Big Wayne was to him.

Surprisingly, he took her hand as he walked her around. She was quiet, basking in the roughness of his hand yet soothing way he massaged her tiny fingers against his.

She was in awe not only with the work that was done with the place, but how much detail Petey remembered as he pointed out things only she spoke of to him. She was in love with this man, she didn't care about the money or lack thereof, close to stopping and kissing him.

Petey was almost there with her, reaching for both hands as they both smiled at each other. It was the perfect moment until they both heard a sound heard Big Wayne clear his throat, making her almost piss on herself.

"Want to tell me how long you been fucking my daughter?" Big Wayne asked him, shooting him the look of death.

CHAPTER 11

"*F*ired?"

"That's what I said," Pepper's manager said, Ms. Harris said, scribbling in her personnel file.

"But why?" she asked on the verge of tears.

"Excessive absences," she said, dropping her pin on the file.

"Look," she said, blowing her nose. "I came in Monday and Keisha sent me home. Said I could get everyone sick. Now here you are talking about excessive. How fair is that? I'm already missing a week's pay? Drew was sick."

"Not my problem. He's your brother, not your child."

"Oh, you…" Pepper said then stopped, catching herself.

"Me what? Say it. You think your little boyfriend's going to come and get me," she laughed, shaking her head.

She'd been working there long enough to see all the girls lose sight whenever the next big "this or that" athlete came through. Especially Pepper who had "trophy wife from the hood" written all over her.

"I have no idea what you're talking about?" she replied, standing up quickly. She hadn't talked to Ishmael in almost a month. She chose to work in the back, doing inventory and washing dishes just to avoid him.

Sashay had covered as much as she could, even giving her a way to sneak out if he hung around the cafeteria afterwards. She had no use for a man like Ishmael, feeling that this was now her karma for the way she treated him.

Especially when she researched himself. He was like a basketball God, ESPN and social media eating him up like he was a three course mean plus desert. He was there on a full scholarship, and even if he wasn't, his family could have paid for it from what she could tell.

She even caught a few interviews where he mentioned his mother, thanking her for being a strong woman, his backbone. She wasn't any of that, hoping he'd just move on. Now he could.

"Well, look at this way," Ms. Harris replied lowly, leaning in closely. "You can always apply for unemployment. Then stay home and collect that check along with the other checks your kind gets."

"What other checks? And my kind" Pepper asked, slowly walking up on her.

"Well, the kind that means my tax dollars pay for you."

"Your tax dollars? Bitch, what the fuck do you mean?" she snapped, all in Ms. Harris's face. "Oh, I know what this is. That old pussy not getting you the looks you're used to getting, huh? Not getting you smacked around the face and mouth with a dick."

"Did you just imply I'm fucking with students? And sucking dick?"

"Nope, I didn't imply, bitch. I said it. And I know why you're pressed about me and what the hell I get coming in. Especially here when it comes to these young athletes you begging to fuck you. They see all of this," she said, feeling herself as she gave her ex boss her back, looking over her shoulder.

"Well, how dare you!" she fussed, standing up herself as she gasped.

"Naw, how fucking dare you. You have to get rid of what you believe is competition when I don't even want them. Any of them."

"Now what would I be competing with? Someone who can't even stick to a schedule, always have an excuse as to why she can't come to work? Yeah, right. I'm definitely so not competing with you," she said with a smile, crossing her arms.

"You know what? You're right," Pepper said now facing her. "To compete, we have to compare, be on the same level and bitch, it's simple. We're not, old dog pound pussy self. So, here you go," she told her, tossing her campus work identification card and key on her desk.

"I think I just might take you up on that offer of unemployment. Gives me more time to lay around and fuck before you do," she laughed, holding in the tears that threatened to fall.

Pepper was tired of being picked on and overlooked, but staying there would cost her more than a job. It could cost her her freedom, because staying there any longer could mean jail time for her if she bust that old bitch in her mouth.

"Figures, I'm not surprised," she said and smiled at Pepper was the one that crossed her arms now.

"Why are you so evil?" Pepper asked, her nose now running as tears began to fall.

"Oh, this is not evil. This is me doing you a favor," she told her, walking so close their were almost breathing on each other. "This is all I have, but you," she said with a soft grin. "You can have more. Don't think for one second these athletes are taking you home to mama. No, dear. They won't. I've seen it semester after semester. You think they are so into you until the next girl's ass is a tad bit bigger and fatter."

She looked down at Pepper, envying how she still looked in a pair of Walmart khaki pants that hugged her ass and a black uniform polo top.

"Don't waste your time, Pepper. And don't think that Iceman guy wants you. Just ask him about Sashay, your friend," she said and grinned. "Saw him all in her face every chance he got."

Sashay had no interest in him, but she was being nasty. But she didn't know why Sashay was talking to Ishmael, disgusted that she tried to pit two friends against each other..

"To ask him about any woman means I actually care," she lied, caring that she was out of job more than him talking to anyone. "Now, may I go now or do you need more time to decide if I should whoop your all old ass or not?"

"Bitch, bye," her ex boss replied with a slight roll of the eye, smiling. "The paperwork will be in the mail. Make sure you fill it out or lose out. The choice is yours. And whoop my ass and you'll be locked up. Guess that's like home too, huh?"

"Fuck you," Pepper told her, snatching her purse from the chair as the tears began to fall.

By the time she hit the hallway, she could barely see, her stuffy nose running now. The cold just lingered, coming and going but now it was worse. She lost weight, barely eating since she didn't have an appetite and now she was queasy and light-headed.

She was all out of honey and lemon, now just drinking tea. All out of money too, Carrie selling the last of their stamps off their EBT card and keeping most of it to herself before she did. Today was the first day Pepper felt almost normal, only to come in and lose her job.

Walking out into the cold air, Pepper heard a group of kids laughing. She wanted to tell them to shut the fuck up. Especially since she had nothing in life to smile about and she would too since one of them was Ishmael.

"Aye," he called out, watching her walk out and right past them. "Yo, Pepper!" he said, trying to catch up with her as she sprinted across the walkway.

She was moving quickly, going in and out as the students were scattered throughout the courtyard and walkways. The faster she walked, the more light-headed she became. Everything around her soon became a blur, but not for long as she soon passed out.

❧

"*H*ow is she?" she heard a woman say softly, her eyes still closed as she wondered where she was.

"Still sleeping?"

Her eyes popped open when he responded, snatching her out of her sleep.

"Ahhh, there she goes," an older, dark skin yet beautiful woman said she now knew was a nurse. "You have been out for quite some time, young lady."

Trying to sit up, she tried to swing around until the IV stopped her along with two strong arms that belonged to the man who couldn't seem to mind his own business.

"Yo, Pepper. Where you think you're going?" he snapped, mean mugging her.

"Home. What time is it?" she asked, coughing.

"Not time for that. Chill, ma and lay down," he told her with an attitude. She could barely get her thoughts together but she knew being there wasn't good for her and definitely not Drew and Blake. Then he called her ma, making her want to scratch his eyes out.

"I can't," she said pinching her lips as she saw two of him, her vision blurry now. "Got to get home to my brothers," she said, looking down as she tried to find the easiest way to remove the IV from her arm.

"Oh, no Ms. Murphy. You can't do that," the nurse said. "You came in unconscious and very dehydrated. Fever a little over one hundred. I'm sorry, but I can't let you do that."

"Well, tell me who can," she shot back, wishing Ishmael would release his hold on her arms. They were big, callous yet beautiful, feeling the coarseness against her skin.

"And you won't have to," Ishmael told the nurse. "Man, you can barely sit up. How do you plan on doing anything?"

"I—I got to get to my brothers. Make sure they are okay," she said as she tried to wiggle free of his hold.

"I can do that, but stop playing. Anybody that can't take care themselves, can't do shit for nobody else."

"I'm fine," she managed to see, slowly giving up the fight as sleep began to set in.

"No, you're not. This bronchitis is serious, ma," he said, softening his voice. He'd been sitting there for two hours, pacing around outside until he had the courage to come to the back. The knot on the back of her head looked like it hurt, but he was sure it was the reason she was on painkillers.

Reaching on the side of her head, she moved just a little but not enough to where his hand didn't touch her. Instantly, she closed her eyes tightly taking deep breaths.

"Fucked your head up with that fall," he said in almost a whisper. She was still beautiful to him, lightly pushing the braids that fell out of her face. He knew she would be mad once she found out they cut a few plaits to treat her, but nothing would change his assessment of her natural beauty.

"Yes, a concussion. Another reason you need to rest. I'm Casey. Your nurse on duty today. Let me go get the doctor and thank your friend. It's a good thing he came with you when he did," she said, giving him a warm smile.

Pepper could barely see, but just the sound of Casey's voice caused her to frown. Ishmael caught that and laughed, but not for long as she casted her eyes his way.

"And it's two thirty," he told her.

"I…" she paused, trying to sit up again but couldn't. "The boys."

"The boys?" he asked, wondering what was really up at home or if these were really her brothers. He too did his own investigation online, seeing her call them her brothers but he wasn't so sure now. Plenty of chicks looked young with teenage kids.

He figured there was more, but Sashay wasn't giving up much shit, and honestly, he was glad she didn't. Now he could ask her himself. Especially since he had practice in about an hour and a half.

"My brothers," she mumbled, her words now fading away as sleep begin to set in.

"So, not your kids?" he asked to clarify.

He never fucked with a girl with kids, but she would be a first. He knew it, too, ready to see about them if she did have any. She shot him a weary yet confused look, but did manage to shake her head no.

"She'll be fine," the nurse said. "That medicine has kicked in, so she's sleepy," she said, adjusting the IV drop.

"Yeah, I hope so," he said, stroking her the top of hair as he scratched his scalp. He looked like shit, his hair needing a haircut as his hair grew long. The part that is he wore in a ponytail was outrageous now, bundled all up in a messy knot.

He wasn't sure what to do next, but he had to do something. He had to with the way she was more worried about her brothers than her own well-being. Before he second guessed himself, he got up and reached for his keys.

"If she wakes up, tell her the boys are fine," he said, not even knowing their names. He figured he'd worry about that once he got to her spot. For now, she was where she needed to be. "I'm about to step out and check on them."

"She's so lucky to have you," said the nurse, rubbing his shoulder. She had no clue who he was and he preferred that, already wearing shades when he came in. The last thing he needed was a headline that college superstar basketball player came into the ER with a bruised and knocked out woman. "I have her. Take your time."

"That's just it," he said, raking his hand through his curly hair on top. "I got practice, but let me get moving. Here's my number if she wakes up," he told her, jotting it down on a nearby hospital menu.

When he walked out the door, Ishmael felt the weight of the world on his shoulders. He didn't sign up for any of this, hoping to come to school to smash some pussy and win a championship. But somehow, Pepper was changing his plans.

He once heard that while people make plans, God makes decisions. Following God's lead, he hopped in his truck and pulled off slowly. He clearly had some kids to go check on, not knowing what he was about to run into. After harassing Sashay who picked up the cafeteria phone after putting him on hold for five minutes, he was on his way.

Knocking on the door a third time, Ishmael was about to leave. It was already a little after four and he had practice in less than an hour.

"Why the fuck—Oh, hey," the older woman said, relaxing her body as she opened the door enough to reveal her body. Her face was cute, he could tell in her younger days many said that, but her body had to have seen better days.

From her eyes and cheekbones, he could see the resemblance to Pepper, but that's where it stopped. Her hair was pushed back off her face, thinning out around the edges and her teeth were stained but not from coffee. He knew from what, knowing a fiend when he saw one.

"What's up?" he said, looking over her head to see who was inside.

"How can I help you?" she asked, pushing the door wide open now to help him look inside.

"I'm here for the boys. Something came up with Pepper, so I came through to grab them for her. She had something planned," he lied, looking at her ashen light skin, her body rail thin.

"Oh," she said, backing up as she crossed her arms. The satin robe she wore was short, exposing she was naked underneath. Even if there wasn't much to see, he could tell she was trying to show it. "What, that bitch done finally ran off, pushing her responsibility off on you?"

"On me?" he asked, now confused. "I thought these were her brothers or better yet, *your kids*. Ain't you her mother?"

"They are but since she wants to play like she's running shit, their hers. I let the bitch do it all since she wants to. Now," she said, approaching him with lust in her eyes. "I can handle this for you before you check on them," she said, sliding her hands to where she easily could feel his massive manhood even though it was flaccid.

"Bitch, you better back the fuck up," he growled, pushing her against the door. When he did, he heard a voice he recognized from behind. It was her ex, someone she briefly mentioned to him.

"Bitch nigga, you better move around and leave Miss Carrie the fuck alone!" Bone snapped, stepping to Ishmael with his hand on his heat.

"Gladly," he said, shoving her out the way as he walked inside.

He was fuming, moving so fast, he forgot his own heat in the truck. He wasn't about to catch an L today and it was too late to back down, taking a walk down to the hall to where he assumed led the bedrooms. One push of the door and he saw the boys weren't there. When he got to the other door he assumed was her mother's room, Bone was on one, questioning Carrie about him being there.

He heard she'd got dropped off one night by someone who clearly had the means and influence to step on his toes. He had been in love with Pepper since before she gave him the pussy, knowing she was too good for him, but seeing a guy of Ishmael's caliber fucked with his mental hard. He'd lost her once. He'd be damned if he let a rich, college kid, hood or not, take her away this time.

"What the fuck you doing?" Bone snarled, as Ishmael made it back to the living room. Carrie stood behind him smiling, enjoying the showdown, too.

"Bruh, I'm telling you that this shit is not what the fuck you want."

"Oh, I want it. It's you that don't want it," Bone laughed, eyeing Ishmael up and down. He dripped with money, his shoes easily costing a grand.

"Listen, because of Pepper, I'm going to leave peacefully, but the next time might not end so well for you, home team. I'll have to push your whole fucking cap back. Then all the bitches will see are your memories, the last when you chose to fuck with me."

"Fuck nigga, what?" Bone spat, aiming his glock in Ishmael's face.

"Alright, home team," Ishmael fumed. "You got that." When he did, he had a sinister smile on his face. "I just was popping in to check on her people's."

"Well, the last I checked, I'm her fucking peoples. Don't come up here showing the fuck off like you 'bout that life. This right here the slums, the real world, nigga."

While Bone was calling his gangster out, Drew and Blake walked inside, calling out for Pepper.

"That's the first one you call when your mama right here?" Ishmael heard her say.

"Oh, hey mama," Drew said, easing up to her slowly. Blake just shot her a look, then dropped his eyes. Ishmael could tell he wasn't feeling her at all. Neither was Drew, but out of the two of them, he determined he was the peacemaker.

"Yeah, Drew. I am your mama. Tell Blake's ass that, coming all up in here like it smell like spoil milk. And if it did, blame that bitch," she spat, roughly wrapping her robe around her body. "Bone, let their asses leave with him. I told you to stop chasing that bitch. She was cheating on you the whole time."

Ishmael almost lost it, eager to reach out and snatch her mother up, but the two sets of eyes belonging to who he now knew were her brothers, Drew and Blake, stopped him.

"Yeah, that's what you say," Bone said lowly as he retreated. "Drew? Blake? Tell Pepper to get at me and soon," he told them, tucking his heat in his waistband. "Yo, Carrie? I'm out. I'll check on you later."

"You do that," she replied, wishing he would stay and fuck her.

Bone carefully backed out, tossing his head up in the air. "Be careful, college boy," he said and grinned which was short-lived. "Until next time."

"Fuck you," Ishmael told him, watching Drew and Blake look between the two of them. Once Bone was out the door, he caught Blake grinning.

"Hey, I'm sorry about—"

"You're the Iceman, huh?" he asked, cutting him off as he got excited. "Basketball player from Miami, right?"

"Boy, that ain't him. You so stupid," Drew fussed, pushing on him.

"Don't be pushing me, fool. I know who this is." Before the boys got into a full fledge debate, he stopped them.

"Hey, hey," he laughed. "It's cool, lil man," he told Blake. "I'm the Iceman, but call me Ishmael. What's your name?" he asked Blake, extending his fist.

"Blake," he said excitedly. "I knew you was coming to Duke," he told him, his fist hitting Ishmael's at the same time.

"You play?" Ishmael asked him.

"I do a little something."

"A little is right," Drew mumbled, eyeing Ishmael with squinted eyes.

"Boy, fu—I mean, shut up," Blake said, catching himself.

Ishmael fought hard not to laugh, covering his mouth. "How about we all just chill?" He reached over and patted Blake on the back, giving him the eye as Bone and Carrie watched on. "I'm here for your sister. She's not feeling well. Told me to ride through and check on y'all," he said, looking around again.

The place was clean, but bare short of the sofa, table, and items in the corner he assumed belonged to Pepper. He didn't have much time and since it was obvious their mother gave no fucks with the look on her face, he decided it was time to clear it.

"Sick, huh? Or pregnant?" she laughed, trying to get Bone all riled up.

"Sick," he replied, not liking her vibe at all. He wasn't sure when Pepper would be out, but something told him to stepped out and just take them. He remember many days going to Nana or his aunt Iyana when his mother was going through hard times, hating that feeling. He was loved, but no kid deserved being mistreated and Carrie looked like she was full of shit.

"Aye yo, pack a bag for a few days. Y'all coming to my spot until she feels better."

"To your place?" Blake asked, his eyes wide and bright full of excitement.

"Yeah, hurry up," Ishmael replied, grinning. He could tell he and Blake would do just fine. "And Drew, you too."

"I'on know who he is coming in here calling shots," he heard Drew mumbled under his breath but took off when Ishmael gave him that look again. He laughed when he did, shaking his head. They reminded him of his bad ass brothers and sisters.

"I guess you just gone keep on talking, huh?" Blake told him, shaking his head. "This is Pepper's friend and if she sent him, that means we got to respect him, Drew."

"Yeah, you're right," Ishmael heard Drew say. "I wanna go, but what about mama?"

"Fuck her," Blake replied lowly, quickly tossing his stuff in a duffle bag.

"But she'll be alone or worse," he said, thinking about God knows who that might come to give her "her fix" as Pepper would say. One day Carrie was a drunk. The other days she was a crack or pill head. She just jumped from one thing to another. Everything but getting clean and back on her feet. Bone swore he'd never serve her, but Pepper wasn't so sure. It was another reason she'd distanced herself from him.

"Like that mean shit," Blake said, zipping up his bag that was already busted on the side. "We coming!" he called out to Ishmael.

"So that's it? You come in and take people kids?" Carrie asked him, hating him more and more by the second.

"Taking or holding shit down for Pep while she needs me."

"Naw, taking but Bone will see you around like he said." Carrie grinned like the evil bitch she was. "I know, baby. She still fucking him, but I guess she fucking you too. Good taste."

Ishmael shook his head, yelling out, "Come on, y'all. Let's roll." They barged out of there, pushing each other like they always did but laughing. *Damn, I got my hands full*, he thought to himself, but surprising, he felt good about it.

He had no clue what would happen next, but if it were up to him, neither Pepper nor her brothers were coming back here.

"Hey, tell your mother you will see her later." He might have not liked her, but she was still their mother.

"Bye, mama," Blake said, side hugging her while Drew gave her a big kiss.

"Yeah, yeah. Bye, boys. Tell your sister we got some unfinished business when you see her."

She rolled her eyes, and walked off before they could even leave. As he pushed them out the door, turning the bottom lock, Ishmael said a silent prayer.

God, I don't know what you're doing, but it's got to be all you. Help me do what you want me do before I mess it up and fu—I mean mess this ole woman up. Amen.

CHAPTER 12

"*D*addy, what are you doing?" Mercedes asked with caution.

"I'm just fucking with you, boy," Big Wayne stopped and laughed, patting Petey on the back. "You know I already know Kimani would beat your ass."

"Kimani?" Mercedes asked quickly, looking at Petey.

"Yes, baby. This lil nigga call himself being in love. I'm surprised I was able to pull him away to get this done for you, but consider this an early Christmas gift. We still have a few things to do, but Petey was on it. We have to a get a marketing plan going, website and all. I know nothing about that really when it comes to this business, but I got something lined up," her father said, motioning for them to follow him.

Mercedes wanted to curse Petey out, but kept her cool as her heart broke into pieces. The entire time her father spoke, pointing out different features he added and why, Petey could barely look her way. Big Wayne was more excited than Mercedes now, not even paying attention to her silence.

"Damn, this your mama," he said when his cell rang, looking at it. "Let me take this, but you like it, baby?"

She didn't even answer, a scowl on her face as Petey rubbed his hand down his mouth. He wanted to curse Big Wayne out, but he didn't. Kimani didn't mean shit to him, but in his opinion, Mercedes couldn't be mad. She'd played him in the background for a long time, hoping she remembered that before she started something that could mess them up for good.

"You okay, Mercedes?" She looked pale now, even shaky like she was on the verge of falling over. "Baby?" he asked, grabbing her by both shoulders, getting her attention.

"Oh, yes, Daddy," she said with a tight smile, looking his way. "Still shocked. That's all. Plus, I haven't eaten much today. Watching my weight."

"This girl stays watching her shape," he told Petey, looking at his cell as Paris called again. "Just like her mama. Damn, here she go again," he said, walking off as he answered her call.

Once he was out of hearing distance, Mercedes snapped.

"Who the hell is Kimani, Petey? And don't you fucking lie to me?" she snapped, unsure how much more she could take. Paris had been poking at her since her breakup with Ishmael and now this.

"No damn body important," Petey fussed lowly, looking over his shoulder. "Let's walk." He slipped his hand in hers firmly, hoping she wouldn't put up a fight.

He had too much riding to have not only Mercedes upset with him, but Big Wayne too. He loved Mercedes with all of his heart, but Kimani was an easy shoo in. A decent front and less of a headache if he were being honest. He'd done a good job keeping the two a part but now Mercedes would be all up his ass.

Kimani was older, already established and she didn't come with the baggage it came with fucking the boss's daughter. But at the end of he day, she still wasn't his heart beat. No, that was all Mercedes.

"How about we not," she fumed, snatching her hand away. "We promised each other, Petey. We promised."

As her voice trailed off breaking, he sighed, reaching out for her.

"Come here, baby. Don't do this. Look around," he said, reminding her that this moment was about her. "I did this for you. Showed up and made sure everything you said happened. She's a situation, one I'm wrapping up. Big Wayne introduced us. He was umm…" he said, not wanting to put Big Wayne's extracurricular activities out there.

"And that means what? He cheats, so you should?" she asked, crossing her arms.

"Me cheating? How when it was you about to run the fuck off? Come on, baby. Please don't do this. I'll handle it. Shit, honestly, it really already is. She mad as hell all my time been working for your dad, then getting this place taken care of." He didn't mention the side work he was doing for Chello, especially since that was slowing down. He wasn't sure why, but he took it as a sign to get out while he could.

Still, Mercedes felt played. She sniffled, turning away from him as he followed her.

"Hey, it wasn't me that wanted to keep this a secret. I've been ready baby. That bitch hasn't even seen me," he countered, pulling her into his body. "Look," he said, trying to show her his cell. Kimani had been blowing him up, but every free moment went to Mercedes.

With a slip of his other hand behind her back, Petey quickly went in, kissing the crook of her neck.. She smelled good, so fucking good to him. And when he looked in her eyes, they were like an ocean he wanted to fall and drown in. Kimani was definitely a good catch, but Mercedes was the prize.

"P—" she started and stopped once he stole a kiss.

"Don't take my heart from me," he whispered against her lips. "Don't do that to me, baby girl. I will dead that…tonight. In front of you if you want me too."

He kissed her once more, his lips resting on hers as he moaned. They felt like pillows to his soul. He hated she was so young, but the heart wanted what it wanted and his wanted Mercedes. "Please, Mercedes. We're this close. Let me talk to her."

"I…" she said, dropping her eyes full of emotion. She wasn't sure what she wanted him to. Especially since Myriah had reached earlier, wanting her to stop by.

"Don't do that, baby," he told her, lightly touching her chin as she gazed up at him. "We both fucked up from the beginning. I sat around and watched you fall for dude, all the while keeping my situation on the low. But have you ever seen me show that bitch around town, all on social media, Mercedes? Has she ever been to the house with me, any family gatherings or anything? Come here, baby. This me. This Petey. Give me some time to let her down easy.

It's the holidays and I wasn't sure what we were doing. But on God, I got you. I got us. That's Big Wayne seeing the love I have for you. It's hard trying to hard it, baby. So fucking hard. I swear that's what it is. He doesn't want me with his baby, but too late. We're here," he assured her, watching her give in as she nodded just a little in agreement.

"I put a lot of work and time into all of this for you. Let me show you more. You believe in me, baby? Don't let this all go over a woman that just held the spot down so ours wouldn't blow up?" he asked, getting in her head as he kissed her once more.

When she heard Big Wayne's voice coming back, she cleared her throat, pulling away. She wasn't so sure if Big Wayne was really on to them or not, but Petey was right. He deserved the same time he gave her to fix things and because maybe, just maybe Myriah was about to give her some good news.

"Just don't fuck me over."

"I can't. You're my world, Mercedes."

"Stop babying her, Petey," Big Wayne walked in, laughing. "I swear we have this one so spoiled."

"That," Petey said, agreeing. "But she's worth it."

"That she is. But let's make a move. Paris reminded me we have to finalize the holiday party for the restaurant. Any takers?" he teased, hoping he didn't have to go with her by himself. Paris was full of shit, but she had an eye for detail and great with party planning.

"Uh, that would be a no, daddy. Finalizing anything with mommy can be a nightmare."

"Word? Damn, Petey, Mercedes ain't loyal at all to nobody," he teased, unbeknownst to himself how true that was. "Well, anyway.

Take her home for me. We'll hook up later at the sports bar. Got something else lined up for that. Mercedes," he said, grabbing Petey by the shoulder. "This lil nigga making big moves but he still came here faithfully to get this right for you. Love you, man," he told him, meaning it.

"Preciate that," he said, giving Mercedes a look that melted her heart. "And I got her. You know I always do. Love you, too."

"Oh, what's the name of this place?" she asked before her daddy was out of there. It was covered up when they pulled up.

"What you mean?" he laughed, looking at her father. "Mercy Me, right? We talked about it."

Damn, I love this man, Mercedes thought to herself, nodding her head. "We did."

But until Kimani was gone, she wasn't throwing all her eggs in one basket. Big Wayne caught that interaction, but said nothing. He still needed to handle Paris about the stunt she pulled this morning but something told him he needed to watch Petey and Mercedes, too.

She wasn't like Paris, but some of her ways were. He'd hate to kill Petey behind his daughter if she fucked him over, but he would with no hesitation if she did something to make him hurt her back.

ब

"*L*ook, don't open the door for nobody. Y'all stay in this room, too. Pizza and wings should hold you until I get back. I'm already late," he told Drew and Blake, opening the door.

"Boy, where you went?" Reno asked him as soon as he opened the door, frowning when he saw the two young boys in their spot. "Yo, you joined the Big Brothers Big Sisters Program?"

"Funny," he said, pushing past him with Drew and Blake smiling as they looked around. "Situation happened earlier. I know their sister. They'll be here until we get back. You good?" he asked Reno, not really giving a fuck if he wasn't.

"Hell yeah, I'm good," he said, wondering what girl he knew that would be so quick to leave him with two kids. They weren't small, but they weren't old enough to be left alone on some college campus.

"A'ight then," he told him. "Go wash y'all hands in my bathroom. It's that way and take off your shoes. I see y'all like to avoid sidewalks, running through grass and dirt instead," he laughed. He hand to run behind them too as they headed towards his building.

"Sorry, Ishmael," Blake said, then took off. Drew just smiled, still skeptical but figured he had to be okay if Pepper trusted them with him. He didn't want her fussing once they finally got to see her.

When they were gone, Reno stood there smiling.

"What, fuck nigga?"

"Pussy, that's what," he laughed.

"Yo, I haven't even had sex with the girl. Just helping out, that's all," he said, not ready to talk about anything else.

"I'm just saying, though. You making some serious moves for a girl you don't even know if her pussy banging or not. That's the chick from the café?"

"Man, shut the fuck up," he fussed lowly, looking towards his room. "And yeah, that's her. I'll tell you about it later."

"Un huh," he told Ishmael, giving him a look. "But they can stay as long as you need them to. Seems like their situation must be pretty bad if you're risking your spot here."

"Risking what? I need a few days. If it's a problem, say that shit. I'll grab a hotel room or something."

"Naw, it's cool. If anyone who know they're here bitch about it, we both leaving this bitch. Where I come from, loyalty means everything. We cool, so I got you. Just keep them crumb snatchers on your side, my man. They in there tearing your room or something," he said, chuckling.

"Damn, let me get them," he said and laughed, yelling at them both.

"But you gone be late on your own, fool," he said, dapping him up. "Those suicides will be all on you."

"Fuck you, " he smiled. "Some things just worth it, you know?"

"We'll see, bruh. We shall see."

He asked himself what would Keyz or Chico do if they were him.

The *old them* would say "fuck that girl and her problems". Especially Keyz while Chico would have tried to fuck her before he did. But the fathers he had now would do exactly what he was doing.

That was stepping up to the plate and holding her down. He didn't have to know her. He just had to know he could help, so he did.

CHAPTER 13

"You ou didn't have to do all if this," Pepper told Ishmael. She was discharged her a few days later, staying back and forth between the home and his place with the boys almost three weeks now.

Thanksgiving had come and gone, her cooking for him almost better than his aunt and mother. They were devastated when he told them he was going home with Reno. It was a lie, but one he chose to tell to give them a happy Thanksgiving.

Pepper "put her foot" in those greens like his grandma Nana would say. Her sweet potato pie was the shit, too. And her turkey. Oh, man, he was in Turkey heaven. It was tender and juicy, loaded up and stuffed with the best stuffing he'd ever tasted.

Life was good and not just for her. He made it seem like a smooth ride, not only getting the boys to and from school on an Uber, but purchasing them more winter attire, sneakers and getting them a haircuts.

His was beyond amazing to her, an answer sent from God. When asked why he was being so nice to them, he replied, *"Because someone would have done it for me and my siblings if needed. So, why not do it for y'all?"*

She wasn't sure what he was used to growing up, but no one did shit for free or without motive where she came from. Still, she accepted his answer for now.

"It wasn't nothing to do, Pepper. The boys are straight. Rowdy, but I'm used to it," he told her, somewhat offended. He was tired of having this conversation, wishing she would just let it go.

They were at school now, so he decided to pick her up and take her to the mall for a job interview. Carrie was knocked out sleep when they went in to grab her shoes, so he forced her to pack a suitcase with more stuff for them while they were there.

Everyone was hiring at the mall, so she put in a few applications, getting a call back from Bath and Body Works and Target. He wasn't sure if he wanted her working holiday hours, but what could he do? So, he shut his mouth, respecting her hustle.

"You're used to. So, I guess not only taking me to the hospital, and taking care of the boys, but getting my cell turned back on is nothing, but you're right. Silly me to actually think you had to do any of that, but thank you," she said, listing each one on a finger as she spoke.

"Yeah, pretty much and silly you," he said with a shrug, turning the music up to ignore her foolishness.

He wasn't in the best of moods, still thinking about his mother's call earlier that day. She had plans on top of plans for him, for the holiday. Knowing her, probably a Love and Hip Hop Miami pilot episodes. She recently hired an agent to book a few gigs for him since he used to rap for fun. After a few underground singles popped up, she was adding "mamager" to her list, but he wasn't having it.

If it was only about family, he would entertain her hands down. But he knew Myriah. She wasn't up to something and one thing he never did was lie to her. So avoiding her was a must.

And then there was Pepper who was...fucking extraordinary. Yes, that's how he described her. She was kind, selfless, funny, grateful, and wanted nothing from him at all, yet he wanted to give her everything at the same time. And would if she shut the hell up.

"Fine, Ishmael," she said, raking her fingers through her hair. He paid a girl to not only come and take her braids out, but wash, blow dry and flat ironed her hair like the Dominicans did in Miami.

Her natural hair was thick and healthy, flowing down her shoulders with body. This time with golden highlights. When she tried to pull that "color don't look good on dark skin girls" stunt, Ishmael shut her down. He told her if she could wear blue with braids, she could wear bold with her real hair.

He made sure she gave his girl a color that would pop, shutting shit down as she shook it lightly, smiling at herself in the mirror. Pepper was effortlessly beautiful.

He was so hyped when it was done, he was about to post a few pics on the Gram just to show her off, but thought against it. Sooner or later, he would but for now, he wanted to enjoy her all to himself.

When he caught her pouting, choosing to say nothing, he felt bad. But she was doing something to him that money couldn't buy. That was making him into a real man who went hard for others, not just for himself.

"Look," he said and sighed, turning the music back down. "For once, just accept things for what they are. Everyone's not trying to fuck, Pepper. I'm digging you hard. I fuck harder with your brothers." He licked his lips and smiled when he did, grabbing her hand.

"Oh, you fuck with them even more, huh?"

"Yup, at least they idolize me," he admitted and laughed. It was "yes sir" and "no sir" all day now. Something those rug rats back home would never say. "Don't hate, you little mean ass girl."

"I'm not. I actually think it's kind of cute. It's just so, so new and different," she replied, trying to hide her own smile. "They'd never had that, Ishmael."

"Cause I'm new and different, baby girl. Not like them lames you used to look to have in their life like that."

He already did his homework on Bone. He was a fucking low level, lowlife wanna be dope boy. He had Keyz look into it, not wanting to put Chico in his business. He trusted his father, but Myriah had a way of getting him to tell on himself sometimes. He and his uncles secretly called him "tender dick".

His boy Blooney had an uncle who used to run the Carolinas. He knew the crew Bone used to run with, too. They weren't making too much noise, but Blooney was ready to take a ride too, but Ishmael was a man. All he needed was information and he had that for now.

He also took advantage of the long ride, eyeing her thick ass legs too. She was wearing a cream color pair of slacks and black top with black boots. He had an eye himself for fashion, knowing what he liked to see his woman in. It didn't take him long to grab her a few things, smiling as he soaked her up with his eyes.

She noticed too, breaking out in a smile. "You know that's creepy," she told him, scooting over as she leaned against the door.

"I'll be that. Keep playing with me, Pep. I'll push your little ass out that muhfucking door," he told her, ready to snatch her over to him.

"Whatever," she mumbled, turning her head away as she smiled even harder.

"So, it's whatever, Pepper?" he asked, reached over and grabbed her hand again.

He surprisingly lifted it and kissed the back of it, not caring that he was falling. She didn't have shit to offer, but here he was vying for her attention. He was territorial as fuck, but he didn't care what she said. She was about to bow down and accept his position in her life.

"Ishhhh," she squealed, turning her lip playfully when he leaned over and gave her a quick peck.

Oh God, I'm falling. Don't let him hurt me...us, she added to her thoughts, thinking of her brothers. In no time, he was like a father. Somehow, the boys fell into a new routine with Ishmael, listening to him quicker than her.

While they went off to school after she fed them and got them on the bus, she'd go to the library and apply for jobs online all day. She was getting worried, secretly prepared to sneak off and go back home. Every time she tried, Ishmael would pop up midday, looking for lunch or just to chill with her.

After good conversation and her going over his homework she was now doing for him, he'd ask her what's for dinner. And just like that, she abandoned the thought of leaving there... and him.

"Boy, pay attention the road," she said breathlessly, trying to get out of her head.

"Naw, pay attention to me," he said, his firm voice as he looked back to the road, still holding her hand. "We are doing this, understand?"

She paused, then took a deep breath.

"Pep?"

"Yes, Ishmael," she said, giving in. "I understand."

"Alright then. And your boy, Bone," he said firmly, lifting one brow. "That's dead, friendship and all. Don't fool yourself about me only fucking people up on the court. These hands can do more, just don't make me," he warned her.

As he talked, she zoned in on his golden brown eyes and pink lips. His warm, butterscotch complexion was flawless. She could look at him all day. *So fucking sexy,* she thought and grinned, pissing him off as he felt she took him for a joke.

"Alright then," he said to himself lowly, done with talking. "It's a joke."

"Ishmael, it's nothing. That's Carrie that keeps him around, but I got you."

"Oh, so now you got me?"

"Actually, I do. So, whatever you got going on at that campus, on the internet, those www sluck buckets, or even back home, how about you dead that on your end, too," she quipped, feeling a bit cocky herself. She saw the comments on post, women asking him if he remembered them from this club or this city. She even saw his ex, Teresita. She was definitely not shy, posting all kinds of subliminal messages that told everyone how she knew him and his body parts very well.

"Girl, the hell you say?" he laughed, clapping his hands.

"Yup, I can threaten your ass, too. Now come over here and give me a kiss. And that's done even though there was nothing there. Bone's feelings are more hurt than anything, Ish. You know men."

"I do and he's a fucking boy. And no, nasty girl. No kissing. You have an interview in fifteen minutes. Get your mind right."

"Ugh, I hate you," she said, kissing her teeth.

That's impossible, he said to himself. *Because I think I love you.*

"You got that, ma," he said out loud instead, popping the locks to the door. He so wanted to say he loved her, pausing as he took a deep breath.

"What?" she asked, getting a little concerned. She thought they'd made it official, but maybe they didn't, wanting to know before she announced it to Sashay.

"Nothing, Precious," he said, kissing her hand.

"Uh okay, but can you do one thing for me?" she asked apprehensively.

"It's whatever, Pep. I'm listening." He rubbed her hand once more, his lips landing on the back up. She grinned, but took a deep breath. She was entering into unchartered territory, but with him, she would do it.

"I need you to pray for me. Pray that this is, you know, God's will."

"I said anything for you, Pep. So, let's do it."

"Thank you. I—"

"Naw, that's enough. Let us pray," he stopped her, pulling her to him. "No doubting or talking. Just bow your head, crazy girl. He got us."

It wasn't a Sunday morning sermon type prayer or Wednesday night bible study one for that matter, but it was perfect.

"Amen," he said that followed by her.

"Thanks, baby."

"Oh, I'm baby now. Damn, the big homie touched your heart."

"Ishmael, you can't talk about God like that," she laughed.

"What? He is the big homie. Listen, we box God in. He doesn't. I'm not religious, but I know he knows my heart. So, when I don't know what to say, I just say what comes to my mind, then let the rest work itself out.

Ishmael wasn't a Jesus, bible thumper. But whatever he had learned during church services and Sunday School, somehow had kicked in. Or maybe it was those Daily Bread devotional pamphlets he got each month. It took him no realize that a praying grandmother,

mother and aunt didn't hurt to have either. He needed it too since he hadn't taken the time to find a church home since he landed up there.

"It's just that easy?"

"It can be.

"I like that. I guess you would call that faith."

"Has to be, Pep. Well, that's what my Nana would say," he said to her, realizing he wasn't the same man that gave his heart to Mercedes. He couldn't be because he had never felt this before.

Pepper was fucking infectious. He wanted to grab her and tongue her down right there, but didn't. They were having a "God" moment and he liked it. So much so, he did something he never did with a girl or anyone else. That's believed that God answered his prayer right then. She was his answer.

"Just feels weird, is all," she whispered, looking towards the mall. Fear tried to set in but he wouldn't let it happen.

"Nothing's weird about trusting God. If you can trust me or try to, try trusting him," he suggested.

"Okay," was all she said as he pulled her into a hug.

"You got this, baby. And congratulations. I'll be out here when it's over. Then we'll celebrate."

"I would like that a lot, but what are we celebrating?"

"Us."

She had no clue what God was up to, but she was walking by faith truly for the first time, willing to follow this man she believed God had sent her.

CHAPTER 14

"You are so wrong for this," Iyana told Myriah as they walked they walked into Home Depot.

They had two weeks before Christmas and hadn't even started with finalizing their Christmas theme for decorations. Each year the did something different. One year was Charlie Brown, another year was Baby Shark. Especially since they both had little ones now, starting practically all over again.

"Wrong for what, Iyana? Wanting to make sure my baby doesn't get caught up with some hood rat? First, that gold digging bitch and now, a charity case. Oh, hell no," Myriah said, grabbing Chizon by the hand who was kicking at people who walked by. "I should have made Chico keep his butt, " she fussed.

"Girl, you know these kids is their way of keeping track of us," she said, putting Kaison in the buggy she pushed it. "Ain't that right Kazzy baby," she cooed, kissing her cheeks.

"I'ma just let Chizon run off and get missing for a few hours. Some damn body will bring his bad butt back, begging me to take him, "Myriah giggled as her son shot her a mean mug.

At two, he was already protective of her, but just bad. His father had him trained, teaching him early on to defend himself but forgetting to tell him his son he could not terrorize others.

"I'm just saying, look where we come from."

"We were born in the hood, yes. But Nana and Papa B didn't play. We were not hood ass kids, sis. There's no comparison. I was out there because I wanted to be out there, but not because we weren't provided for, had rules and what not. So, it's not the same."

As Myriah defended her position, spying on Ishmael through a paid investigator, Iyana knew this wouldn't end well. From the footage she saw, she was pretty proud of her first baby since he was the first born out of all of their kids.

He basically did what she would hope her own children would do if someone was in need. The girl looked a tad bit rough in terms of how she looked and where she lived, but she never once saw her behaving as if she had no tact or manners.

"So, what do you plan to do? Hypnotize him over the phone so he tells you," Iyana teased.

"You know I never thought of that," Myriah said to herself, stopping to grab a batch of scented pinecones. "Chizon, stop it!" she fussed, watching him pick up two and toss them at people walking by.

"Sis, put him in the buggy," Iyana giggled.

"Hell no. His long ass. His behind is going to walk."

"And harass people," Iyana added. "And when someone wants to smack his butt, Kaison and I will walk off like we don't know you or this little booger," she said, pinching Chizon's cheek.

He tilted his head, and batted his eyes smiling when she did.

"Chizon, if you are good for auntie and mommy, I will buy you anything you want today?"

"A spaceship! Yes!" he cheered, slapping a nearby Santa display.

"Do it again and I'll slap you to the moon, boy," Myriah fussed, grabbing him. She scooped down and picked him up, trying to put him in the buggy. He caught her neck instead, hugging her. When he did, he kissed her cheek hard, then pulled back and smile. Myriah melted immediately, kissing his nose.

"Guess he's getting two spaceships," Iyana said, watching Myriah's mean butt forget all about being mad.

"He's my baby. Ain't' that right, Chizon?" she said, lifting him up and sitting him down. "So long, just like Ish was."

"Exactly. Size fourteen shoe in the making. I swear between Ish and Keyz, I don't have no shoe space in any of my closets. That child of yours has the same pair in every color. Then I come to your house and its like looking in the shoe department."

"Exactly. His first endorsement I know will be a Nike one, too. You think I'm letting that fast tale girl get her claws into that?"

Iyana chose to let her vent, grabbing a few white lights for the driveway. She loved a more serene setting, going with white and powder blue to decorate the outdoor area no matter what theme they finally came up with.

"Iyana, when KJ gets old enough to date and possibly make money like Ish, you will see."

"Actually, I won't care. As long as my baby is happy and is treated well, why would I care where his girl comes from? My husband is an animal and whole street dude. Yours too, but I couldn't imagine a life without Keyz, sis," she stopped and said, grabbing her hand.

"So why isn't he telling me about this girl?"

"Maybe the same reason why you are judging her. I know why Mercedes rubbed you the wrong way. And honestly, her mother is to blame for that. That's all Mercedes knows. To be a pretty arm piece and secure the bag through the form of a mate.

But honestly, I think if we spent time with her, we would see a different side. You never gave her a chance, sis, and now you are about to go FBI on this one I'm sure Ish has his reasons for spending so much time with."

"Ish got him a bi—"

"Boy, if you don't watch your language!" Myriah said, covering Chizon's mouth.

"Nana already made him eat soap before," Iyana said and laughed. "He pooped for two days. You remember that?"

"No way. Are you serious?" Myriah asked in disbelief, grabbing

Chizon by the head as she looked in his mouth. She then leaned him against her chest, hugging him tightly. "Oh no, Papi," she said, hoping he wasn't devastated. "No wonder he hates bar soap."

"Oh, sorry," Iyana replied, covering her own mouth this time. "That was supposed to be a secret."

"Hmph," Chizon said with poked out lips, as he looked her way.

"Nana is crazy for real," Myriah said, shaking her head. "Like, psycho. Who does that?"

"Girl, whatever. She is no crazier than you are, but she really didn't. Just stuffed a bar in his mouth until he cried. He's so stubborn, so he started chewing on it first, then she took it out. Now, that's crazy!"

"Hey, need I remind you KJ likes to cut up Cree's clothes. A serial killer maybe, sis," Myriah shot back, giggling.

"Whatever. It's just clothes," she said, waving her sister off. "But anyway, we have to find a balance. You didn't have any growing up, doing what you wanted and now you're overbearing. That boy needs space."

"That boy needs his head checked out. He's smart, talented and a go getter. I made my mistakes so he doesn't' have to. Why am I being looked at as being so bad?"

"Because your mistake turned out to be perfect. Ishmael is not a tragedy and whatever happens with this girl will not be one either. Give him some space. Don't interfere," Iyana pleaded, gently rubbing her back.

"If I don't, it might be too late," Myriah mumbling, feeling defeated. He dodged Mercedes, but that goofy look she saw in his pictures with Pepper made her sick to her stomach. She couldn't let miles, hormones with some girl and wild parties with more girls be his story. No, she just couldn't.

"Just don't push him away, Myriah. Ain't' that right, Chizon?"

"Nope, I like pushing," he growled and laughed wickedly, tossing his head back.

"Girl," Iyana mumbled, shaking her head. "It's this one you need to watch."

"Yes!" he cheered on, none the wiser as he knocked a few items off the shelf. With a pop on his hand, he howled while Myriah ignored him. "These damn kids are getting on my nerves."

"And you are getting on mine," Iyana said more to herself, watching Chizon grab a bottle of glue and open it up. "That one right there... whew, you can have him."

❧

"Well, hello there," Myriah said, opening the door for Mercedes. She still couldn't believe she'd gotten a call from Myriah. She was sure she knew why Ishmael had broken it off with her.

"Hey, how are you?" she asked, walking in cautiously. She wasn't sure if she was about to be hit across the head or not, knowing Myriah could be a tad bit off from the stories she heard.

"I'm doing well. Come on out back. I'm sorting out old clothes. Things the kids can't wear anymore or just won't. Even me. Especially that older son of mine," she eased in, watching Mercedes eyes stretch a little when she did. "A little trouble between the two of you?' she asked, cutting to the chase.

"Uh, trouble? Why do you asked?" she probed, clutching her purse. She wore a pair of distress jeans, boyfriend style, and a white-tee that hung off her shoulder. She'd been designing most of the day, dropping everything when Myriah hit her up.

"I don't know. Maybe since you didn't ride up with us and all this time, you haven't visited. Although I did hear you went by my sister's," she said, handing Mercedes a bin of clothes to go through. "Here, toss something I should just toss and fold up what's worth giving away. If you see a tag on anything, hand it to me. Those will go to the unemployment program for young mothers."

Mercedes was impressed, hearing how humanitarian Myriah was. She was rich, but far from bougie. She could tell she was genuine, not batting an eye at a jacket she knew easily costs four hundred dollars. If nothing else, she knew fashion.

149

Her earrings clang just a little, causing her to laugh nervously as she grabbed on to them. "Sorry, a new pair I designed."

"I see. I heard you had a thing for that. I'm impressed."

"Really?" the young and still impressionable, beautiful girl replied.

"Of course I am, " Myriah said, feeling bad this was going so well. She still didn't care for Mercedes, knowing her mother's DNA ran through her veins. Paris was a hood rat with makeup, a boob job and money.

"Wow, I just…" she said, her voice trailing off. "You know I had been trying for a while now to apologize for not being what you expected me to be. I know you don't like me," she laughed, fidgeting with her fingers.

"What? You thought I didn't like you?"

"Yeah, it was pretty obvious, Mrs. Ramos," she admitted, shrugging her shoulders.

"Nonsense. Just protective, that's all. I'm sure Paris is, too. And the apology, well let's just say none is needed," Myriah slipped in, watching Mercedes in awe as she held up a pair of "fuck me" boots she owned. They were on the floor along with a bunch of other shoes. "Love those."

"Yeah, they're pretty hot," Mercedes confessed, never recalling Myriah dress so edgy. "And these," she grinned, looking at the thigh high, leather boots.

"Are mine too, believe it or not. But I rather not even go there," Myriah laughed, not even wearing them two times. Chico took one look of them and banded his wife, from stepping out the door with them. She got them to wear with a edgy t-shirt dress and tights on a trip to London with the girls.

"You actually have amazing taste," Mercedes said, tossing them back to the side. "Not for the unemployed unless they are working," she teased, but made it sense once Myriah thought about it. "And working for quite some time. Then, they deserve to kick back and wound down while spending a night out on the town."

"Yeah, I suppose. So, Ishmael? Ready to talk? I need all the tea," Myriah laughed lightly, hoping this different approach would work.

Myriah refused to like Mercedes no matter how much she seemed to be into their little project. She wasn't fond of Teresita who let Ishmael walk over her, but even she would be better to control than this mystery hood chick.

"Honestly?"

"I wouldn't be asking now if I weren't, Mercedes," she almost snapped, catching herself.

She didn't have much time. She sent Chico out with the kids to get a few items for the homeless shelter. It was their turn to host Thanksgiving dinner this year. He had already called a few times fussing, so she knew he wouldn't be gone too much longer.

"I sort of messed up, wasn't sure what I wanted."

"Oh," Myriah said with a frown. She was stomped for a second, confident before it was Ishmael that messed up. He was a man. Usually it was always them. "How so?' she probed, the wheels churning in her head.

"Just an old situation. Someone I shouldn't have been dealing with in the first place," she laughed, feeling her heartbeat quicken as she thought of Petey. "He's like my first love. Well, a first of everything for me. You know how that is," she said, this time looking in Myriah's eyes. "Just silly and young, I suppose."

Myriah noticed they were sad. Eyes that were almost a mirror to a younger version of herself. Eye she once possessed when she didn't know who she was or her worth, growing up. Eyes that hated who she saw, destroying two best friends with a baby in the middle of it all. That situation was one for the books, making her squirm just a little even now as she thought of it.

"And did my son know? Like before you got caught?"

"He knows him somewhat, but we weren't really together," she answered, short of saying they were back together now. Or trying to be. "I just didn't end things well, I suppose." Her voice trailed off, leaving an uncomfortable pause in the air.

"Hey, you ever wanted someone but didn't go all in because it was forbidden?" Mercedes asked, that gave her courage to push that pregnant pause out with a question.

"Once, but this isn't about me," she said quickly, clearing her throat. "So anyway. Any thoughts of reconciling?"

"Please," Mercedes laughed. "Do you know how stubborn and cold-hearted your son can be? I don't think so." He'd got those traits from both parents. Myriah was still surprised he came out to be such a noble young man in spite of the two of them. Even with God in their life.

"I do, but it's all a front, girl. He's not that much different then most men. They break up with you, cut you off and then go crazy, out there in the world sleeping with this one or that one. Silly stuff. It's not to be taken seriously," she said, unsure if she wanted to send that message or not.

Mercedes frowned, not seeing him in that light at all. The blogs only showed him on the court. A few photos revealed him leaving a few parties and a strip club, but nothing that said he was being a whole hoe out there. If he were, she might have felt some type of way.

The ones that showed more, Myriah quickly paid to have them removed. She didn't want him to know she was on to him, and thankfully, neither was Mercedes. They both were a pawn in her game, a game she had to win.

"My mother has said that before. You know the men will be men stuff. My daddy's not like that and if he is, he does a good job of hiding it," she laughed, hoping Myriah didn't know anything to add truth to that.

Girl, if you only knew. Big Wayne was exactly like that back then, she thought to herself, laughing. As far as she was concerned, Paris deserved whatever Big Wayne did to her then and now.

"Yes, Big Wayne has been known to be pretty nice back in the day, but he's a saint now," Myriah chimed in, lying as a fake smile plastered her face. "Quite the pair, and that Paris is something else," she said with a smile.. "Never a dull moment with her and quite the business woman."

"She is, but she's my mom. And well, my dad has accepted her ways I guess," Mercedes admitted, not realizing she confirmed her mother was a whack job. "They both just want me happy. So, if we could at least be friends…Ishmael and I, that would help me sort of move on," she said, looking at Myriah with pleading eyes.

Myriah felt like she was taking candy from a baby, reaching over and hugging her. "Ahhhh, it will be okay. Maybe that's exactly what he needs because girl, his current situation seems a bit suspect to me. A friend from a familiar place just might be the answer."

"Situation?"

"Yes, you have time?" Myriah asked, leaning over like they were the best of friends.

"I sure do. I am all ears."

"Good, because I need some help. He's the big shot on campus and all, barely calling his mother. Hmph, imagine that," she said lowly, grabbing her cell to show her.

"Wow, Mrs. Ramos. I'm so sorry he's doing you this way. I thought it was just me."

"Nope, but I definitely know who it is. Look," she said, going to the secret photo gallery she had in her cellphone from the investigator she hired.

"You know I was scared when you called me," Mercedes admitted, letting her guard down even more. Since Myriah had made it so easy for her, she was ready to let it all down.

"Water under the bridge," Myriah said dismissively. "Focus and check these out." Mercedes looked her through squinted eyes, wondering who was this black heifer he was all booed up with. Then she moved on to a few videos that made Mercedes see red.

All this time Ishmael made her feel like a piece of shit, ignoring her efforts to apologize. Now she was fuming, seeing he was doing exactly what his mother said he was. To add insult to injury, Pepper was a bad bitch. She would say cute, but cute wasn't filling up jeans as nicely as hers did.

Sadly, Mercedes couldn't find one flaw, but she knew one thing. This bitch was from the projects. She knew project money on a person when she saw it. Money given and money earned and from the looks of it, Ishmael had picked up a hood rat, sponsoring a whole life-style to include two kids.

"Started kind of young, didn't she?" Mercedes huffed, giving lots of attitude that Myriah could appreciate

"I know, I know," Myriah said and sighed, patting Mercedes' hand as he wrapped Pepper all up in his arms. He looked like he was sickly in love, gazing at Pepper in a way he had never gazed at her before. And with two boys following right behind them.

"Ugh, I bet she says skrimp instead of shrimp. Probably don't even know what surf and turf is, but can follow a Popeye's chicken sandwich in her sleep through a snow storm. Girl," Myriah sang, raising her hand in the air as she waited for Mercedes to high five her which she did.

She did, but she wasn't happy at all. She was sick of men. Ishmael, Petey and even her father for bringing Petey in her life. She was done. Done, done and all of them would feel her wrath, starting with Ishmael.

"You ready to get your man back or just your friend? Myriah asked, seeing the disgust in Mercedes' eyes.

"Hmph, you already know. When do we get started?"

"Right after we toast. No champagne since you're not twenty-one, but I think I got something you can toast to," Myriah said and smiled, doing a little dance. She would worry about how to get rid of Mercedes later. Besides, she gave her enough ammunition, telling her about her first love. Bad habits ways are hard to die, but Myriah was all in.

She'd be damned if she let Mercedes or this project bitch come inside her circle. It would have to be over her damn body.

CHAPTER 15

"Yo, Blooney, my nigga," Ishmael said as he hopped in his Tesla. "Thanks for bringing my whip up. Myriah was home?"

"Bruh, you know your pops regulated," he said, passing his blunt back to Kevin. Both were eager to see their best friend, choosing to stay home and play for FIU.

"I know," Ishmael laughed, happy to see his best friends. "Bring your ass inside and meet my roommate."

"You mean your girlfriend. Y'all all cozy in your little suite?" Blooney asked, slapping him lightly on the back.

"Say that shit again, Bernard?" he snapped, calling him by his government name. "I mean, Bernice. You the only nigga that play like a bitch don't run you when she do. Yo, Kev? What that was you told me?" Ishmael asked, outing his boy out.

"Man, why the fuck you bringing me into this?" Kevin said, mean mugging him. "Just say you two miss each other, kiss and go make up for trying each other," he told him, snatching his blunt back when Blooney went to grab it.

"I got something you muhfuckas can kiss," he said and laughed, walking them across campus. He wanted to show them around before they went out that night.

Da Baby was performing at Bojangles in Charlotte. Pepper had to work, refusing to call out, even when Ishmael agreed to pay her a week's worth of pay. She landed that mall job and was easily getting fifty to sixty hours her first two weeks. He told her she had one more week and he was making her quit.

His little homeboys, Drew and Blake, were settling in to their routine coming to his spot three days a week instead of home to do homework and chill, but three days were easily turning into five days.

"Yeah, I heard," Kevin said, giving Blooney that look. They had to hear Myriah say all kind of slick shit about Ishmael not calling or being not being open about how he spent his time off the court.

"Heard what?" He knew Teresita wasn't lying on his dick. After Mercedes turned out to be foul, he shut all his dealings down with anyone from back home. Teresita included.

"I'm just saying, home team," Blooney said, eyeing a group of girls walking by.

He liked him a snow bunny on any given day, learning quickly how they could take a pop quiz right for him right as soon as he popped his penis out of their mouth. He wasn't trying to wife a white girl, but FIU came with perks outside of a full basketball scholarship.

"What's up with the fine ass chick? Dark skin girl? She fine ass fuck, yo," Kevin said, testing his gangster.

"Fuck you know about her?" Ishmael snapped, easing up on Kevin.

"Yo, home team, it's all good. I just asked," he laughed when Ishmael pushed him in his chest. "Chill out."

"Naw, you chill out. What you know about Pepper?"

"Pepper, huh?" Blooney asked as Reno walked up on them.

"Oh, I already knew he would be talking about her. Roomie in love," he teased until he saw the scowl on Ishmael's face. "I'm just play-ing," he laughed, holding both hands up in surrender. "Just came out to speak." He moved past Ishmael, hitting Blooney and Kevin with some dap. He saw them as he came out of the library.

"Well say less then," he told them, bumping Kevin by the shoulder as he walked past him to his apartment.

"Is he serious?' Blooney asked, wondering why he was tripping so hard. There was plenty of ass for him to get over the next two days, so arguing with his boy was for the birds. They'd been up almost twenty-four hours, and still had a full night with the show ahead of them.

"Is he? Mannn," Reno said lowly, giving them that look. "But she cool people though. Body, personality on point. Make sure his home-work straight, papers too. Cook, clean. You name it? And I'm Reno."

"Word, that's what's up. I'm Blooney. This right here is my boy, Kevin."

"Told you his moms tripping," Kevin told Blooney, passing him the blunt as he dapped fists with Reno.

"She said he fucking a slum bitch. Somebody she knows is just trying to get in on his payroll, but you know women and especially mothers. No female is good enough for them. Shit, but if home team's happy, why the fuck she care is beyond me."

"You already know why," Kevin reminded him with that look in his eyes.

Myriah was finer than a motherfucker herself. The streets talked, had been talking. She was hell back in the day until she found Jesus. Now she forgot her hoe strolling days, minding her son's business.

She hated Teresita, despised Mercedes, but was ready to assassinate Pepper even though she had never even met her. Honestly, she was the cool mother when he was growing up. The coolest out of all of them, so her moving like his was strange. They couldn't smoke, but they could hang out and have girls come through there

Once he started pulling females, even some older than him, Myriah lost her shit. All she saw was her son's life being ruined, even worse than what she felt she'd done in the past.

"Bro," Blooney warned him as they eased into. A quick tour around let them know that a woman definitely had added her touch to the place. Not that it needed much in terms of furniture, but the plants, pictures and pillows all screamed a female marking her territory.

"Well, I'ma get out of here," he said once more, dapping them up.

"Hey, good looking out and for helping him keep his head on straight. I can't call it, but his ass been sweet on the court. Twenty-eight points. I would never have imagined dude raising a whole family up here," Blooney said, still in disbelief.

"Yeah, Ice don't fuck around," Reno said, smiling to himself. "Proud of him, for real."

He overhead Pepper and him praying one night before a game. That night, Ishmael was on fire. The next game, they prayed too as he sat outside the door. He caught himself kneeling down and playing too. That same knight, he had sixteen rebounds, two steals, and twelve points.

"We see," Kevin said with the munchies, opening up the fridge. While their room back home was stocked with the usual college snacks like chips and cookies, lunchmeat and sodas, Ishmael and Reno's was filled to the brim. "Who the hell grocery shopping?" he asked, pulling out a plastic storage container with jerk chicken pasta in white sauce with broccoli. "And cooking? I know you said she was doing something, but this?"

"Yes, that would be her too," Reno said, wondering if he should make him a plate before he took off. He looked at the two of them, knowing the chance of any food being left were slim to none.

"Naw, gone now," Kevin told him. "She can cook for my big ass anytime," he laughed. "Let me see what she got that really has my boy so wide open," he said more to himself, licking his lip.

"Yo, keep looking. Freshly brewed iced tea and banana pudding in there, too. Oh and a leman pound cake."

"Damn, is he pregnant?' Blooney teased.

"Suck my dick, Bloon," Ishmael came out from the back laughing. "I see Reno's ass can't keep his mouth shut for shit. Bitch ass."

He was happy his boys hadn't said anything too foul about Pepper, listening to see if he was going to have to cut them off or not. He shot Reno a look who shrugged like he was confused, then waved him off. He figured these were his best friends. They would find out sooner or later anyway.

"Bro, she seems straight. Hell yeah, his big ass bragging. I say keep her! If she can get you to eat like this and you can get her to cook like this, I'm starting to think if your mother is just a hater," Kevin said, spooning him out a portion of a banana pudding as he sipped on the iced tea.

"My mama? Wait, what the hell y'all talking about?"

"Shit, I guess he didn't know," Blooney said lowly. They knew nothing about the investigator, but the look on Ishmael's face was proof she shouldn't have known anything.

"It's cool," he grumbled lowly, grabbing his cell. He had posted a few pics on IG, mostly just her body or theirs. Last he checked, his page was private, but maybe it wasn't. Changing his settings, he felt shady as hell, but so what. This was proof as to why.

If he had to lie and hide her just to have her all to himself, he would. "Yeah, Myriah in her feelings," he said to himself, looking at a few comments, one being his mother. "Since when did she get an Instagram account?"

"Since you stop calling her all the time, I guess," Blooney said, his mouth full of lemon pound cake. "Oh, and it gets better," he followed up, looking at Kev who's face looked tight, bracing himself for Ishmael's next reaction. "She and Mercedes are cool as hell now. Saw her over there the other day."

"What the hell?" Ishmael said, snapping his head their way.

⁂

"You sure he's coming?" Mercedes asked. Petey tried to make plans for Christmas, but they still weren't in a great place. She even think she overheard Kimani mentioning something about being pregnant. They had broken up, but Petey was moving funny and she wasn't having it.

Over the past few days, she and Myriah became pretty tight. This was the third time she was there, this time coming in with Chico was home. He wasn't too sure why she was there, but he played it safe, choosing to observe and say nothing.

Once they settled in, resuming their clothing donation project,

Myriah gave her all the inside scoop on ways to get back in her son's good graces. Mercedes was sure Petey was where her heart was, especially after he sat outside her window all last night crying, but she couldn't help but enjoy this motherly attention.

Especially from Myriah after all of this time.

"Of course. He won't let me book his ticket, but he's probably driving down. You know Blooney and Kevin took that Tesla up there," Myriah said, rolling her eyes. Chico was in the doghouse for that, but that was more one reason she needed to get that hood chick away from him. She didn't know he gave it to Pepper to drive or she'd kill him.

She was convinced the girl couldn't spell Tesla let alone knew just how expensive it was, scrolling all day on social media to catch her riding in it. She painfully was losing her grip on her son, now getting desperate.

"Hey, baby!" Myriah squealed when Ishmael picked up. Mercedes almost broke her damn ankle running her way when he did. She peeped out the family room to see Chico snoring up a storm in front of the TV. The kids were with Iyana, so it was just the two of them.

After this, they were going over to Mercedes fashion studio to meet up with Iyana and grab the kids. It was her way of giving back, creating Christmas costumes for Iyana's annual Christmas play she led each year. Iyana was forced to sit with her the day before, hating how fake Mercedes could be.

She did think Mercedes was talented, but this was going way too far and she wanted no parts of it.

"Nothing much," he spoke softly, looking over his shoulder. He'd begged Pepper to come home with him after he scooped her up from work. She agreed but only if they boys came, so they didn't get in until close to one in the morning. "What time is it?"

"Well, I would say time to go to church but since I hear no tambourine or clapping in the background, I guess it's just time to just get your butt up works, right Ishmael?" she replied sarcastically.

"Ma, please," he groaned, sliding out the bed and out the bedroom door. The boys were on a queen air mattress on the floor right on

Pepper's side. Drew was doing his usual snoring and Blake drooled a pool of slob down his face. "Why you not in church?"

"The kids are with Iyana, you know for the Christmas play rehearsal she puts on every you. I have to prep for that, costume stuff. Oh, and food. You know I feed all the kids and parents that come out."

Ishmael smiled remembering the Christmas play his himself used to be in. He went from being Santa to the Snowman, even the Grinch one year. He loved acting, which led to him rapping too. No year was the same, but she always seemed to slip in a scene with Mary, Joseph and baby Jesus.

"Word? That's what's up," he said, going into the kitchen. Thankfully, he didn't have to cook since Pepper made two quiche for him he didn't eat the morning before. That girl could start her own restaurant, easily fitting into his family.

His mouth watered eyeing the vegetarian one filled with bell peppers, tomatoes, green scallions, and cheese. The meat lovers one could be for the boys, stuffed with chorizo, bacon, and sausage.

"Any who, there's someone here that wants to speak with you. Now, before they do, remember how I raised you. You're already moving funny, as you kids like to say these days, but I will deal with you later."

Before he could protest, a half a second from hanging up, Mercedes hopped on the line.

"Ish," she said softly, her voice so sweet and smooth. The same way she was when she cooed in his ear. He loved her voice, still did as he clenched his jaw, but still hated her at the same time. "How are you?"

"The fuck you want, Mercedes?" he muttered, being careful not to wake Pepper up.

"I—"

"Apologize right now," he heard his mother say in the phone.

"Damn, I'm on speaker?"

"No, you were loud and try me again, Ishmael Payne. Try me one more time and see," his mother threatened, ready to snatch his head off. "I am still the mother, Mister Celebrity, King of Basketball," she fussed.

"Ma, come on now," he fussed lowly, peeking around the corner. He thought he heard a door opened, but didn't' see anyone there.

"Never mind," he heard Mercedes say in the background.

"Aye, I'm out, mom. I love you, but you're fucking wrong," he told her before he disconnected the line.

"What?" Mercedes said, close to tears.

"What is me kicking this up a notch. Keep the tears rolling. I have an even better idea."

Unfortunately, Pepper woke up, hearing Ishmael outside of the room. She wasn't sure who he was talking to, but whoever it was, he wasn't too happy. Stretching, she yawned quietly not, wanting to wake up the boys.

She was off today, hoping she could sleep in just a little longer. Before she closed her eyes, she reached over and grabbed her cell, logging into her work group chat. Sashay was working there now for the holiday season, starting it up.

It was called *Carolina BBW Bitches,* the BBW for Bath and Body Works. She giggled, watching a few associates go mad crazy about the managers. One girl, Leeann, told them she was calling out, hoping anyone of them was willing to take her hours. Not Pepper, quickly leaving the group.

As soon as she did, a friend request popped up. She was a very pretty girl, someone who seemed to have a lot in common with her when she looked at her profile, but no mutual friends.

Assuming it was just someone Facebook recommended because of that, she accepted her and then logged off.

"Let me see why this boy is in there fussing," she said to herself. She heard pots banging and doors slamming which meant his mood was really bad. "Especially if he insists of waking up these boys," she grumbled, easing out of bed.

She just didn't know she accepted the same person that pissed him off—Mercedes. She changed her look, darkening her hair and adding tons of makeup as she prepared to do more than just be her Facebook friend.

She plan to ruin Pepper's life.

CHAPTER 16

CHRISTMAS EVE MORNING

"*I* got something," Solomon told Myriah, eager for that wire to come through. "I mean this is really something." Solomon worked for *The Shade Room*, but had a crush on Myriah. She never fed into it that much, but he quickly took her up on her offer to ride up to North Carolina.

When he got there, landing on his target, even he could see with Stevie Wonder's eyes why Ishmael was so enthralled with Pepper. He would be too, but money talked. So, he was ready for his payday. The few thousand she'd thrown his way so far were a good side hustle, but this could set him up to start his own spinoff of the *The Shade Room*.

"Something as in she's just with a guy, that can't easily be explained?" Myriah whispered, walking out of the room. It was family night, movies, popcorn, hot chocolate with pillows and blankets.

The kids were all set up and Chico has just joined her. "Damn, Myriah. Don't take all night now. Talking ass women," he fussed, checking his own cell. He was wondering where Ishmael was, but would hit him up once the kids went to bed.

Storm and CJ were being nice, their Christmas list shorter after slapping each other around while Chizon had no list. He was bad as fuck, unbothered after opening up gifts in the middle of the night earlier in the week. The Christmas tree was tilted that morning too, earning him an ass whooping.

"Oh, let's just say it's better than that. It's definitely pornhub action."

"No fucking way," she said excitedly.

"Yes fucking way. It's dated, so it doesn't look like her now but it's her, Myriah."

"Send it," she said quickly, hearing Chico call out to her once more. "I have to go."

"Send half and not the usual. I want twenty-five," he said, as in thousand dollars.

"Twenty-five!" she fussed, covering her mouth.

"You want it or not, Myriah? The blogs already want to know who she is. I can get more from—"

"Fine. Sending it now. When I do, I want everything you got," she said, hanging up in his face. She swiftly went to her secret Cash app icon and sent the money. When she came around the corner, she smiled.

Her husband was so fucking handsome. She couldn't believe after everything they'd been through he was all hers. No more cheating, no more lies and no more scandal. That's how she justified everything she was doing now.

This along with Mercedes next move would seal the deal.

"Bring you're a—I mean butt here," he growled, pulling her on his lap.

"Can somebody tell these old people to get a room?" Storm said, rolling her eyes.

"Right. Just nasty," CJ said, sticking his tongue out like something nasty was in his mouth.

"Nasty got all three of you here. Ain't' that right, Chizon?" Chico said to his youngest son.

"Yassss," he said and laughed, throwing a cup at CJ that hit him in the head.

"Argggh!" CJ hopped up, ready tackle him.

"Don't. I got him," Chico said, grabbing Chizon. "He'll just watch us eat while he don't," he said and smiled. "And drink water."

"Don't do my baby like that," Myriah laughed, while Storm rolled her eyes.

"I hate them... all of them," she said, twisting her lips. "Can we replace them with dolls instead? Their so annoying."

"That's you all day," Chico chuckled, gripping on Myriah's thigh. "We're in trouble, baby. Big trouble."

We will be if I don't get rid of that hood rat, she thought to herself and smiled.

"Yes, dear," she said out loud instead. "Yes, we are."

ॐ

"*The* *world is in a frenzy. Ishmael 'The Ice Man' seems to love more than basketball these days. He's loving porn stars...*" the *Shade Room* reported.

"*She's a beauty, but look at all of that booty...*" *TMZ's* headlines said.

"*Oh wow! He has balls. Big ones...*" E! Online posted.

Social media was in a frenzy and Myriah was grinning as each headline flooded her timeline. She had just found out Ishmael finally made it to town. He surprised her with a morning call, wanting to come over before the kids got up. She could tell he had no clue what was buzzing, rarely did he unless she told him. And today, she preferred it that way.

That was her job as his informal manager, eager to show him once he showed up. She knew it would crush him, but he would recover. He was built strong, formidable—just like her. If she survived and was now living on top, even with all the cheating Chico had done to include their paternity scandal, so would their son.

"Yes," she laughed, logging onto Instagram. Mercedes just made her post.

"*Coming in three months. Who would have known?*

165

#ishjunior #Imstillbae #neverduplicated #imthatbitch #babypay-neonetheway #hoodbitchwho

And she was looking like a million bucks. Ass on display, even in a nice soft pink jumpsuit she designed herself. Myriah hated Mercedes, but her stepping up and stepping in like the champ she needed her to be was making her think twice about what was up next.

She had her own insurance policy, knowing the baby wasn't her sons if she were really pregnant. They happened to take a test, but Mercedes was a mini Myriah. She had dropped a few fake pregnancy test on people back in her hay day, so she assumed Mercedes was no different.

Sadly, it wasn't. Mercedes found out the day before she was pregnant. She just wasn't telling Myriah or anyone how far along. The six months was just to get under Ishmael's skin, but the pudge proved that she was indeed carrying.

Paris assumed it was college weight gain, that Freshman Fifteen they liked to call it. And it was, just with the help of a baby. Myriah was in full swing with mode, dancing and prancing around until she heard the front door open and close.

"I'm hommmme!" Ishmael yelled out. It was like Mayhem, the kids running in from all direction, including Chico.

"My boy!" Chico said, grabbing him and pulling him in for a hug. "Nigger, I know you was already here," he whispered in his ear, smiling. Ishmael was him all day. "Can't fool your pops."

He knew his wife. She could be a handful. He wanted to check Keyz for not saying shit, but he remembered he loved Ishmael just as much as he did. They would forever have to share him, so he fell back, choosing to love on his son. That late night munchies attack put him across town right through Keyz's neighborhood.

At first, he wanted to stop, but he decided to chill. He knew something was brewing. So staying focus to watch his wife was way more important.

"Dad, what you talking about?" Ishmael replied, feigning confusion but smiled as he slapped hands with his father. "Just needed a breather, you feel me?"

"Shit, do I?" he mumbled, slapping him on his back. "Hey, y'all let him inside," he laughed, bending down and picking up Chizon.

"My nigga," Chizon laughed, throwing his head back when Chico tickled him.

"Oh God. Get him, Ish. He's so rude and hood," Storm said, with her little hands on her hip.

KJ was half sleep, standing there smiling as he rubbed his eyes. He'd been playing video games quietly while the others slept. He was paying for it now, but happy to see his big brother.

"Can you all let my child go so he can see his mother?" Myriah said playfully, yet teared up as he stood in the living room.

He was her whole heart, her reason for getting her life together. Even going to church and seeking a life pleasing in God's sight. She still had her moments, her current scandal as proof, but no one could ever say she didn't love her children. Especially Ishmael.

"Bro, she better not be pregnant," he said to his dad, shaking his head. "All emotional."

"Yo, she stay emotional. Don't blame it on that."

"Got to hell," she fussed, rolling her eyes at her husband. "Come to mama."

"And on that note, let me go grab your stuff. She's been on one, son. I need a break," he told him, taking a deep breath. "Come on CJ. Walk it off. And next time, there wont' be a video game to sneak and play. I let y'all assess think I don't know the game. I created it," he laughed, while CJ pouted.

"So, you finally came home to see your family?" she asked, falling into his arms. "What, there's no Thanksgiving in North Carolina?

"Ma, it's been what, three or four months? I'm hooping, killing the game. You see the headlines. The Ice Man is doing his thang, Myriah. And yes, I did it in Nevada," he said, reinforcing his lie.

"Call me Myriah again and The Ice Man is going to have a sore ass. Don't play with me, boy," she told him, giving him that look. "I'm short but these hands got reached," she said and laughed, amazed he was a foot taller than her. "You're hungry?"

"Yeah," he said, sighing.

He begged Iyana not to cook so he could have a full stomach when he made it over there. She even helped him buy tickets for Pepper, the boys, Sashay, and her son. Even agreed to host them at her place, too.

Once he couldn't sleep, he got up and went in the living room, sitting in front of a silent TV that played re-runs of *Love and Hip Hop Atlanta*. He hated shows like that, but it seemed to be what everyone else liked, chuckling every now and again as he watched Stevie and Joseline go at it.

He had rubbed a good one out, still made she was back home at Carrie's. He understood loving someone who didn't deserve it but it was fucking with him. Then her not driving that Tesla, taking that Uber instead pushed him to the edge.

He needed her to not only love him, but trust him too.

"So, you really like her?" she asked her nephew, her heart swelling.

"A lot auntie. Honestly, I love her. I'm in love with her," he said, quickly correcting himself.

"So why isn't she here?"

He sighed, unsure if he wanted to admit his reason for not bringing her short of work. He knew she could quickly find another job, but it wasn't just that. It was his mother. He knew she would do everything possible to run her off.

"You really want to know, auntie?"

"Boy, it's three o'clock in the morning. Of course, I want to know. Whenever something is wrong with my kids, even you, I can't sleep. I wasn't even surprised to find you out here alone. Now, why isn't she here?"

For the next hour, he told her about Pepper, how they met, and where they are now. She watched an array of emotions pour out of him as he spoke, rubbing his hand, then gripping it when he seemed frustrated.

She knew firsthand how evil her sister could be. They hated each other growing up. Well, Myriah hated her but deep down inside, she knew Myriah had a good heart and was acting out of fear.

"So, what should I do? I already told her I was flying her in? Her and her brothers."

"Then be a man of your word and do that. Live in your truth. I lost fifteen years of loving your father. Keyz was out there giving my good dick

away," she chuckled, surprising him with such a blunt disclosure. She was the prissy sister, the one who rarely cursed.

Myriah had the nasty mouth, but Keyz had a way of making Iyana say some shit that only he could make her say. She loved her husband to no end, and would do whatever she had to do to keep him.

She was educated, smart, beautiful, and talented. She ran a whole dance studio, community center, and several restaurants, but she would give it all up if she had to choose between that and her husband. He wasn't worthy of her, let him tell it, but to Iyana, he made her the woman she was.

Him and her children, from Ishmael to Kaison. They were her life. She would forever feel like she failed him if she didn't step up and help him out. Even with Ishmael who was battling with being his mother's son and his own man.

"Go to bed. I got this. Just give me their information. They can stay here while you figure out a way to tell your mother. And if I know my sister, she won't go down easy, but she loves you. She has to accept who you love or risk putting a wedge between the two of you.

"But why is she like that? Especially when..." he said and stopped, not wanting to speak on his mother's past.

"Unresolved pain is all I can come up with. Myriah loves to pretend all is well. Money and image can do that, but my sister still has some stuff to figure out. Maybe this will force her. I love you, Ishmael. Get some rest. I'll be with you every step of the way."

He was looking at his aunt with so much love in his eyes, even down to her dark skin. She was the same complexion as his Pepper and strikingly beautiful, even shades darker than his mother. He couldn't believe she once hated her complexion.

"What?" she asked him, looking confused.

"My dad is lucky to have you, auntie. He chose right," he admitted, not trying to shade his own mother. Iyana was everything he knew Pepper was and could be.

"Oh, wow," she said, unsure of how to take that. "But thank you."

"Naw, thank you. I really do love you...like a mother. Let me grab a few hours of sleep because I have to deal with Hurricane Myriah," he said and chuckled, getting up.

"Yes, please do. And remember, you must always live in your truth."

"Oh my God!" Myriah said loudly, covering her mouth. She had just put a pot of grits on and slid some turkey bacon in the oven. The corned beef hash was next when she decided to set her plan in motion.

"What?" he asked, quickly getting up. He had washed down a glass of homemade lemonade, ready to eat.

"Ishmael, look?" she said, handing him her cell. She watched him turned red as a beet, his jaw clenching as he scrolled through *The Shade Room's* post. "Is this the woman you have been hiding from me?"

"Shit, it's the same woman that's been hiding from me, too. Fuck!' he said, tossing her cell phone on the counter as he took off.

CHAPTER 17

*I*shmael could barely get in his truck without his cellphone blowing up. It was text messages and inboxes from everyone from Blooney and Kevin to Keyz. He frowned at Keyz's inbox, mentioning Mercedes being pregnant.

"Pregnant? What the fuck?"

Ishmael had no clue what was going on. In the past year, he had it all. The best senior year of his life, wining his high school three state championships, a gang of college offers, choosing one of the top in the nation and now bagging the love of his life. Even after he was said he was done with love after the bullshit Mercedes pulled.

He was done. Done, done.

Back in Durham, Pepper was waiting on Sashay and Fat Fat to show up so they could all head to the airport. She couldn't believe when his aunt called asking for her email address. She was so nice and warm, making her feel like a part of the family.

She hoped she wasn't making a big mistake calling in, but it was now or never. She was tired of second-guessing herself. Once his aunt told her how much he had shared about them and his need to have her there, she was all in.

After getting to the airport, she checked her cell. She had sent him a good morning text and call. Both went unanswered.

"Hmph, that's strange," she said to herself, but figured he wanted to pretend she wasn't coming in. She told him not to buy the tickets and he agreed, so she assumed he was playing tough with her. "Never mind. He's so moody sometimes."

"Well he better get unmoody," Sashay tossed out there. "I already had to step my boost game up. Luckily, the café is closed for two weeks because of the holiday break. But I'm about to hit them streets when we get to Miami."

"Girl, I know you're not talking about stealing?" Pepper said lowly, the kids all sitting with their ear pods in their ears while Fat Fat was sleep. Ishmael bought the boys iPhones, so they stayed tuning her out as they did it all from watching Netflix to STARZ as they enjoyed catching up on *Power* all the way from season one.

"Hell no. Twentieth Street. It's like Canal Street in New York. I'm buying me a suitcase and racking up! Bundles, lashes, purses, boots, dildos—"

"Enough!" Pepper laughed when she got to sex toys. "Enough," she said a second time as she struggled to breathe.

"Hey, I'm the plug, baby. Single bitches need a little love too…like me."

"Please, you are not single."

"Well, if Blooney asks, I am. Have you seen his ass? Girl, I want to climb up and down that tree," she said, pulling out her cell. "Never mind. Let's clear TSA first. That strip down is serious. Ayyye," she sang, sticking and wagging her tongue.

Once they were settled in first class, Pepper took a deep breath and exhaled. Then looked at Sashay. "How do I look?"

"Like a school teacher who's trying to look sexy, but hey, I get it," she said, knowing her girl's struggle with being Ishmael's woman. She wore a dark pair of fitted, black jeans, a softy grey sweater, and gray boots. She threw on her small diamond earrings he bought her as a "just because" gift and made sure her curls were bouncy and full.

She loved her plaits and braids, but her real hair did give her a softer, more mature look. Since it wasn't permed, the humid air cause it to curl up naturally. Although she wore no makeup, her lip gloss gave her look just enough pop to finish her look.

"I actually like this look. Now, Bone would have—"

"Don't bring up that asshole," Sashay told her, showing her the DMs he sent her way, trying to talk to her. "Can you believe him? Even said something about me separating myself from you. That you were a whole hoe. Whatever the fuck that means, yet he wifed you even though it was him that was cheating. And you were what, still a kid?"

Pepper wondered what he meant by that, pushing their entire relationship to the back of her mind. She only had one or two incidents she could vaguely remember. Incidents that required her to do some things she wasn't too proud of.

The details were fuzzy, but enough to know it was something she would never speak on. It didn't matter though. They were close to being homeless with him taking care of his household and hers.

At sixteen she couldn't say no. She wasn't old enough to get a lease herself and Carrie wasn't even concerned the sheriff's office had put an eviction notice up, saying they would be back in seventy-two hours.

The second time he needed to re-up. Tammy never called him back, even after everything he'd done for her ,so he asked her to step up and hold him down like he'd done for her so many times before.

When she got sick from all the pills she took to do it, almost overdosing, he never asked her again.

"I was a kid. And fuck him, girl. He's just a hater. Ain't' nobody worried about nothing I did that long ago," she huffed, crossing her arms.

"Damn right. Huh, Fat Fat?" Sashay said to her her son who's hands were sticky with candy.

"And you wonder why we call him Fat Fat?" Pepper said and giggled, shaking her head. "Let me get some shut eye. I got a feeling this is going to take everything in me to pull off, Shay."

"Yeah, well damn his mother. If that bitch wants the smoke, I'll smoke her old ass. Fuck her."

Pepper laughed, giving Sashay a kiss on the cheek. She was just as hood as she was loyal. She'd stand ten toes down for her girl any day, hoping Blooney would see what she saw. All Sashay had done so far was like his pics, commenting on a few, but once he saw her, Pepper was sure her girl was next.

Yes, they too deserved to be treated like Queens. Why not them?

CHAPTER 18

"Your fucking wife is on my shit list," Keyz fumed as Chico hopped in the car.

"Bruh, I just don't know anymore," he said to Keyz.

"Hell, I know. She almost cost us *us*, man. My fucking brother, my son. After all of this time…" he said and stopped, gripping the steering wheel. "Fuck it, let's go find out where Ish is."

With the way Ishmael took off, Chico didn't have time to stop him. He ran inside, trying to figure out what had happened just that fast. He knew it couldn't about the Tesla since he told on himself, but his excuse was he did after his wife put the pussy on him. He figured it was for his son to stunt and he deserved to do it, so no biggie. He was a boss in his own right. Myriah always did the most, but now he was at a loss. He just couldn't understand why she refused to live and let live.

While they combed through Liberty City, hitting up all the spots they figured he would be, he was sitting off in Blooney and Kevin's apartment on campus. Their spot was almost as plush as his, but wasn't since their apartment didn't come with all the bells and whistles a school like Duke had that catered to their athletes.

"So, you just gone not do shit and hide out, bro?" Kevin asked

Ishmael, scratching his head. He was ready to get fucked up, five bottles in his room with a bag a kush. Even after he had a hangover, the bitch still laid up in his room.

"I ain't' fucking hiding. Shut that shit up. I just need a moment."

"A moment to process you're about to be a dad or you know…" Blooney said, careful not to mention the videos flying all over social media. They didn't look exactly like Pepper, the one he had a chance to meet, but they did resemble her a little bit. "Ish, maybe it's not her."

"That's my bitch. I know her, everything about her," he told him boy, tossing back a bottle of Hennessey. "Fuck!" he yelled, picking up and throwing it against the wall.

"Damn," he said and sighed, looking at his boy losing it. "I know security coming."

"Fuck security," Ishmael said, daring for someone to come and touch him. He was hurting and bad.

"Yeah, well let me go bust another one before they do just that," Kevin said, standing up. "That's fucked up, Bloon. Don't say that shit no more," he told him, wondering why he had to bring it up. He saw a few posts and logged off immediately. He'd be damned if he looked at his boy's ole lady pussy like that.

"I'm just saying though," he said more to himself as he stood up. "You love her?" he stopped and asked his best friend. He figured he knew the answer, but still had to ask.

"Who? Mercedes's sloppy ass?"

"Well, at one point I would say yeah, but not her, nigga. You know who I mean. Shit happens, though. She was like what, twelve?"

"See, no matter what, shit like that shouldn't happen. And if it did, why would she not tell me?"

"Would you tell a motherfucker that you believe may not really want you that at some point you fucked up in your life? Fucked up so bad, the shit is all over the internet, Ish? Bruh, you're tripping for real. That girl didn't even look like she knew what the fuck was going on. Damn, so fucking dumb. Come on now, Ish. You yourself said that's not how she moves. One moment can't define a person forever. I'm just saying. So now it's fuck her?"

"Basically," he said, grabbing another bottle. "And stop buying this cheap ass alcohol," he said, lifting a bottle of 1738. "Live a little."

"Fuck you, Little Bo Peep who lost his sheep…but got a baby on way in a snowman sleigh. Yo, that shit rhyme. I'm a rapper," Blooney shot back and laughed.

"Dumb fucking rapper, too," Ishmael snarled, tossing the bottle back. "Shit's probably not mine. I'ma fuck Mercedes up anyway. How the fuck she six months and I'm just finding out?"

"Didn't you say she was calling and you blocked her?"

"Damn right. She's not my bitch. Why would she be calling?"

"Causeeeee, maybe she is pregnant?" Blooney said, wondering what was really up with his boy.

"Yeah, well she could have told my mother a long time ago. The internet, bro. Sneaky as fuck," he said, taking a seat as he rubbed his hand through his hair. "Dude probably thinks it's his. That Petey asshole. I punched in his shit, yo," Ishmael chuckled, liquor running down his mouth.

That situation with Keyz and Chico fucked him up for a while when he was younger. The last thing he would do is abandon his kid. Even if he didn't care for the mother.

"That could have cost you that scholarship too. Ish, can't you see she's bad news. I don't think it's yours, but the answer is not in that bottle, yo."

"So," Ishmael laughed. "You Dr. Phil or some shit?"

"I'm Blooney, your best friend. Here," he said, handing him a bottle of water. "Drink this and give me that." He snatched the bottle from him before he could protest, daring him to get him. "Chill now."

"I am," he mumbled, looking at the bottle of water like it was poison. It didn't want to think or feel and if he did, he usually took it out on the court.

"Fuck it. Let's shoot some hoops," he said to Blooney. "Tell Kevin that pussy not that good and hurry up."

"This boy losing it," Blooney said and sighed, going to his room to get his ball.

Ishmael nodded, knowing exactly what Blooney was saying. But it all just didn't make sense. He needed Pepper so bad right now. So bad, his chest was hurting.

"And stop reading the fucking blogs. They will be the death of you," he told Ishmael, knocking on Kevin's door. "Hurry the fuck up. Times up. She tired of that fake as moaning she doing anyway."

Ishmael felt better already, busting out laughing as he spewed water everywhere.

"Bitch, clean that up and let's go. I'm ready to body you two bitches out here," Blooney told him.

"Not before I body a muhfucka first," he growled lowly, thinking of Mercedes, Bone, Carrie and for the first time since he met her —Pepper.

CHAPTER 19

"I'm so sorry, honey," Iyana said, cradling Pepper in her arms. They were headed to the Margaritaville. It wasn't her home like she had planned, but there were shops, restaurants, a few Christmas shows lined up and the best ocean view in South Florida.

"But, but—"

"Girl, forget him. If that ran him off, he's not worth you," Sashay told her. "And the boys are going to get upset. No matter what, you are everything to them. And to me after Fat Fat."

Sashay was ready to put hands on Ishmael, while Pepper felt like she was about to die. As soon as they turned on their cellphones when they landed, she had a text from Iyana, asking her to call her. She wouldn't tell her why she was picking her up until Sashay showed her her timeline on Twitter and Instagram.

"He's hurt and confused, but she's right." Iyana didn't want to say anything more that would appear to be her taking sides, but she wasn't too pleased with Myriah's actions.

She knew immediately the video was this so-called private investigator's work. She watched Myriah, most of her life, play victim while stirring the pot. It was a classic relapse move, Myriah up to her old ways whenever she felt like she was losing control.

"How about I drop you all off to Dave and Busters first?" Iyana asked Sashay, referring to her and the kids. "Let me spend some time with her alone."

"Boys?" Sashay asked them, watching the scowl on Drew's face. He wasn't sure what was up, but Pepper crying didn't sit well with him. Blake, usually the more vocal one, spoke up.

"That's cool. Is she going to be okay?" he asked Sashay as Pepper rested her head on Iyana's shoulder.

"Yeah, girl stuff. She'll be fine. And Drew, you hold on to Fat Fat before I beat his butt," she said, watching him take some candy out of Iyana's purse.

"He's fine," Iyana snickered. "I got three at home myself. Kaison just one, going on five like a rough tomboy. A whole mess, girl."

"I like you," Sashay blurted out. "But your sister," she said, squinting her almond shaped eyes. "She can get it. I know she has something to do with this. I know it. Come on, boys," she said, motioning for them to follow her to the Iynana's truck.

They were finally alone, pulling up to Cheeks, Iyana's first restaurant in Palm Beach. It was the smallest out of all of her restaurants, but closest to her heart. It was closed, but Iyana needed to open up before the day got busy.

"Wow," Pepper said as they walked inside. "The name Cheeks threw me off, but this is amazing," she said in awe, taking in the two story restaurant that sat off water. It was a soul food joint with a stand for a live band and karaoke.

"My nickname," she revealed, smiling. "My dimples. My husband Keyz, the other one Ishmael calls his dad, started calling me that when I was like fourteen. Of course it was behind my back, secretly crushing and it sort of stuck."

Pepper noticed them too. Her grey eyes even more. She was told she was a cute to be dark skin but Ishmael's aunt was definitely the embody of elegance and beauty. She was the perfect package, wearing a pair of burgundy slacks and a gold, beaded top that fell off one shoulder. It was sexy, yet tasteful. Her hair was swooped up into a loose ponytail as a few curls dangled around the sides.

"Fourteen? That's impressive. And yes, he told me about it. Not easy to listen to, if I'm being honest."

"I know. Trust me," Iyana said with a tight smile. "And at fourteen, he would have never told me he had a crush. Let's just say we had to go through some tough times to get to where we are, even after that. The paternity, baby scandal. Then with all of social media, it was hard just to live peacefully when that was over. Try googling us. I'm sure you missed a few old articles that might shed some light on our past. Even why my sister is still so....angry, I suppose," she told her, raising her eyebrow.

"Oh?"

"Yeah, but while you do that, let me whip us up something to eat. Chicken and waffles?"

"I'd like that," Pepper said, wondering where this was going as she pulled out her cell.

❦

"I've looked everywhere," Keyz said, sucking his teeth as they sat around at their boy Chello's house. "I want to fucking kill that bitch," he said lowly, while Chico cursed Myriah's ass over the phone outside.

"Myriah's back at it again, I see," Chello said, pouring himself a glass of V-8.

"Nigga, your old ass drinking V-8 now? Where's the Henny, Patron or something? Better yet, blaze up, fool."

"Can't," he whispered, then smiled. "My baby's having my baby," he grinned, Mulan still in bed with Tiana all up under her. At forty-two, he was finally getting out the game. Mulan told him if she was pregnant, it was either she and the kids or the streets.

He was honestly over it, but the news she was pregnant and with a son, he said fuck the game. He was officially announcing his retirement at their annual New Year's Eve party.

"Word?"

"Yeah, man, but she hasn't said anything. You know she's all private, that police bullshit mentality she got. I'll kill a motherfucker that come for me and mine, but until she starts to show, we haven't said anything. Three months now, going on four."

"My man," he said. "I'll fuck with a V-8 then even though it's whack," Keyz chuckled, texting Iyana. When she told him she had Pepper and the others that came with her, he told her he loved her. Then thanked her for holding it down like always.

"So, Myriah's decided to not only be the mother of the year like always, but the crazy mamager, too. I swear her pussy must be have gold in it or something, fam. I would have been cut her off. Don't get me wrong, I like her and she took a lot of shit off of Chico, but when is enough enough?" Chello asked him quietly, pulling out a few leftovers.

Mulan still couldn't cook for shit, so he always went by Iyana's restaurant a few times a week to grab a few things. Mulan had gotten better, but her gas had gotten worse. So, anything he could do to make eating enjoyable for him and then her, he did.

"Aye, that's my wife's food," Keyz smiled, hopping up when Chello placed it on the counter. He knew Iyana's cooking from anywhere. It was her infamous chicken potpie, wrapped up in their specialty box.

"Indeed," was all Chello said, turning on the oven. "Now, what are we going to do about Ishmael? I know it's tough letting Chico take the lead."

"Who said I'm letting hi ass take the lead? Fuck that. I'm letting him handle his wife. He can lead on that, but my son? Naw, that's me. He just with me. I can't trust him to check her and then regulate my son when he has a right to be mad.

Trust, that leaked video is all Myriah. She stay with the shits and giggles. But my son is not a joke. Never was since the day she brought him to me. I raised him like my own, so he's my own.

She got a past way back then, but now," he grunted, looking out the door was Chico was fussing, "she can be a dead bitch."

"My nigger," Chello said and laughed.

"Dead. End of motherfucking story."

"Less, he's still your best friend," Chello chuckled, hearing Chico come inside.

"He is, but she's not."

"You good?" Chello asked Chico, watching his boy look like he lost his best friend.

"Until we find Ish, naw. I just don't know, Chello. I thought..." he said and stopped, taking a deep breath. He was close to tears. The last time when Skebo was shot accidentally by him. He was hard, hard as they come but he was soft when it came to those he loved.

"I know, but maybe this was necessary. We all have our demons and she's been through a lot, some you caused, bro. Let's just relax and pace ourselves," Chello said, looking at Keyz when he did.

"She doesn't get too many more passes from me, yo. I'm saying," Chico said, surprising the both of them. "We promised each other that. I did my shit, my last little situation with Shonasia two years ago. Y'all both know how I feel about Shonasia," he said, referring to one of the female former crew members. He was dating Meka but it Shonasia was the Bonnie to Chico's Clyde.

"Yeah, we know. Heard she and X expecting," Chello slipped in, looking at Keyz who smiled. They wanted to see Chico act up and he did, clenching his fists.

"Pregnant?"

"Twins, they say. You know the ladies talk. Heard Mulan mention it to Sunshine."

"And Skebo ain't tell me?"

"For what? Bitch, you just said you and Myriah promised each other no more passes. So why should you care? Shonasia will always love you, but hey, X is her one. Focus, bitch," Keyz told him, ready to ride over to Myriah's house and knock her the fuck out.

"Well, like I said, if I can walk from Shonasia, she can learn to sit her ass down somewhere. Let the boy live, make his own mistakes."

"Exactly. So you ready to put your foot down or stay guilty for the rest of your life, letting Myriah made you feel like she run shit? It's called forgiveness, Chico. Either she forgives you like you have forgiven her or maybe it's time to, you know, move around," Chello said, hating the advise he was giving.

If anyone wanted him and Myriah to work he did, but not at the expense of Ishmael's happiness.

"Any regrets?" Chello asked him, watching his face go through a myriad of emotions as he thought on what he heard.

"Hell no. I love my wife."

"Well, you got to love everything that come with her. Then hold her accountable. But first things first. What's up with video scandal and a baby? Boy, I swear my young nigga just like his daddies!" Chello yelled, clapping his hands. "Never a dull moment with y'all two."

"Naw, you mean this motherfucker," Keyz snarled, shooting Chico a look. "I'm good over here. I never tried to wife anyone that wasn't wife material."

"Bitch, you talking about my wife?" he asked him, slamming his hand on the kitchen island.

"If your wife fits that shoe, slip that bitch on then. Mine is cleaning up your wife's shit. So watch who the fuck you come at, Chico. Let's not pretend Myriah's innocent. It's been years and she's still creating chaos amongst us. I don't hate her. I swear I don't, but if my son goes off on the deep end and messes his ball career and life up behind her, suit up, motherfucker. We will be in court...if we both make it out alive," he told him lowly, meaning that shit.

"Naw, what we are not doing is fighting each other. This is nothing but the enemy," Chello said, trying to be the voice of reason.

"Whoaaa," they heard as their boy Skebo walked inside. "Did I hear this one mention the enemy?" he asked, walking up and giving Chello dap. "Bible study must be working," he said and smiled.

They all attended the same church, some more than others. Skebo was the first one to be saved, very active in ministry. He'd been down with all three of them since he was sixteen, slinging as much dope if not more when he first started out. He was hungry then and hungry now. Only this time, his hunger was for family and the Lord.

"Dude, shut up," Keyz laughed, extending his fist. "Why are you here?"

"Why else? Sunshine already told me what was up. Myriah called her because your wife won't talk to her. You know these ladies. When one in the mix, they all get caught up in it. We thought you and this fool right here," he said, looking at Chico, was about to kill each other. "Let me tell her everyone is still breathing."

"For now," Keyz mumbled.

"Keep it up, motherfucker. I didn't do shit. I'm just upset as you are. I know my wife petty as fuck. Damn," he said, walking towards the bar. "I need a drink or better yet, a blunt."

"All out," Chello told them, looking at Keyz with a smile. "Mulan's expecting."

"Well, that does call for a drink. Congrats, man," Chico said, grabbing a glass. "And Keyz, for what its worth, if this doesn't pan out well for Ishmael, maybe I do need to evaluate my marriage."

"Word?" Skebo said, shocked as hell. Chico and Myriah had that Bobby Brown/Whitney Houston connection. They stayed on bullshit most of their relationship, finally settling down once Storm was born. CJ and Chizon really brought them to a happy place, but him mentioning anything that sounded like divorce shocked all three of them.

"That's serious," Chello said, pouring him a glass of sparkling apple cider he found.

"Nigga, what's this?"

"It's called happy wife, happy life, motherfucker. Feliz Navidad that. Now, drink up and let's eat. Let me put some eyes on Blooney or Kevin. Something tells me he's with one of them. Crew for life?" he asked them, holding up his glass of apple sparkling cider.

"Crew for life," they all said, clanking their glasses. Chico hoped Chello was right because he was all out of answers.

CHAPTER 20

"*W*hatever you do, never fold until they have evidence," Myriah told Mercedes as they met at her trucking office. It was ghost town there, mostly an industrial area since it was the holidays.

"I have evidence. I am really am pregnant," she whispered, unsure of how she felt. When they came up with the scheme, it was supposed to be all for show, but when she saw the positive sign, the joke was on her.

"Girl, seriously? Shit, I thought you were joking. I have plenty of times," she laughed.

"Yes, ma'am. I really am."

"Damn," Myriah said, shaking her head. She didn't even want to know if it was Ishmael's, knowing she herself carried very small when she was pregnant with him. She had just gotten rid of Pepper but a baby meant ties for life. She hated Paris. Sharing a grandbaby with her sounded like a life sentence.

"Damn is right. I have so much riding on this. My first semester in college, my fashion design studio opening up and now this. I was sure I loved Petey, but now he will know I was up to something with you about Ishmael."

"Petey?" Myriah asked. That named sounded familiar. She couldn't place where, but she would deal with that later.

"My ex or my ex for real now."

"And what does Paris have to say? Counting those commas, I bet. Ugh," she said, taking a sip of her coffee. The kids were with Sunshine, Skebo's wife. After Chico threatened to leave, she had to get them out of there. Him not coming home at all was not an option. At least not one she was prepared to explain with the way Ishmael left earlier.

"Honestly, she is counting the commas," Mercedes admitted and laughed even though she wasn't really laughing. "Ever felt like your world was ending, and like it was your fault?"

"Many times, but look at me now," she said, waving her hand around. They were on the sixth floor, the entire building belonging to them. They rented out the other two unit units for five grand a month. They were eating simply by owning the same building they used for their trucking company.

"But is that enough, all of this?" Mercedes asked, wondering if her entire life would look like her mother's or worse—Myriah's. They both had plenty of money but they clearly were lacking in the area of self-love. Even she could see that.

Shit, I've been played, she thought to herself as she balled up her fists.

&

"Damn!" Ishmael grunted, watching his four heroes coming his way. He loved both of his fathers, but his Uncle Chello and Skebo held him down too when he was young. "Who called them?"

"Hell if I know," Blooney said, stealing the ball and scoring a quick two. "Ten, eight," he said, keeping score. He was up by two. They'd been playing one on one and he was kicking Ishmael's ass.

"Toss me the ball," Keyz said.

"Unc, come on," Blooney said, ready to finish Ishmael off.

"We're starting over. Ain't that right, Ske," Keyz said, motioning for him to join them. "Let these old heads show you how to really kick some ass," he said, tossing the ball as he approached his son. "Sup, son? You ready?"

"Dad, for real?" he asked Keyz.

"I can either whoop your ass on this court or in the streets, Ish. Your choice."

"I'm whooping his ass, period," Chico said, burning one as Chello sat by, waiting to pull on it. He hadn't smoked in a month, itching to get in on the bag they got from Kevin when they went by the apartment.

"Why, what the fuck I did?"

"Talk reckless to me again and I don't care what Keyz say or do, I'm beating your motherfucking ass," he told him, easing his way. "And it's called running. We don't fucking run from anybody. Never have, never will."

"Especially not from our responsibility. You already know I had no clue you were supposed to be mine, but what did I do when your mother brought you to me?" Keyz asked him, tossing him the ball.

"You stepped up," he mumbled, looking down as he lightly bounced the ball.

"Look at me when I speak to you, Ishmael Payne. Man to man, eye to eye. Right?"

"Yes, sir."

"Now, let's go. First one to twenty gets wings for free for life on this motherfucker," Keyz laughed, pointing at Chico. "Fuck that food truck you own. We're eating for free. Close that bitch down."

"Shoot, I got seven little ones at home," Skebo chimed in. "Let's do this. Wings you say?" With a quick steal, Keyz hit a quick left then right, gunning towards the rim with a nice swoosh sound following.

"Damnnn!" Chello choked as he laughed, feeling like an amateur and as he toked on the blunt. "Youngin', that's two!"

"Oh hell, no," Blooney fussed, rebounding the ball. "I, got, something, for, your, old, ass," he said in between bounces, spinning around Skebo who hopped up and slapped the ball down.

"Yooooo!" Chico yelled out this time. "Maybe they need to smoke some of this," he laughed, causing them all to fall out.

They must have played two to three games, wearing Ishmael out. When he was too tired to be mad, they made him make a first call. The first one to Mercedes. The second to Pepper.

CHAPTER 21

"Hey," Pepper said softly, meeting Ishmael in the hotel lobby. He didn't even speak back, pulling her immediately by the hand and into his body. She felt like home, squeezing her tightly as he fought hard not to cry.

He didn't know he was damn near holding his breath until he exhaled the moment he saw her. She started to cry, her body feeling like it as about to give way as he slowly walked them backwards until they sat on nearby sofa.

The lobby area was in full swing. The shops were buzzing and the live band was playing all of the traditional songs from "This Christmas" to "Silent Night". For the first five minutes, he said nothing. Just stared at her, lightly stroking her cheek. She was everything to him, and he'd hurt her by shutting down instead of being there for her.

"Ish, I—"

"Shhhh," he told her, not wanting to talk just yet.

He leaned over and took her mouth, kissing her soft as if her lips were like petals. She tasted like the rainbow-colored candy cane Drew had brought back for her. Her lips, soft and plumped, were consumed by his mouth, their tongues dancing as he pulled her into him. He whispered, "I'm sorry, baby," then held her tightly again.

He was crying. It wasn't a loud, ugly cry but she felt his tears on her face as they fell. They both were water babies as she soon joined in. When he was ready to speak, he let her go just enough so they both could lean back and stare at each other again.

She sighed, then bent down, laying her head lay lazily on his chest. When she did, she felt his heartbeat, which was perfect since she truly was his.

"I was sixteen," she said. "Scared, confused and angry."

He clenched his jaw, not wanting to hear it, but knew he had to. He owed that much to her. He'd be a hypocrite if he didn't. So he took the time to gather himself to give her just that. Especially since he needed to explain the whole ordeal with Mercedes.

"Carrie had just started neglecting us. Well, it started before that but it was obvious then. She went from at least making sure we ate to barely keeping food in the house. And the lights were always a hit or miss. Some months they were on, other months they were not.

Then Bone showed up, you know being really nice, I guess. I would see him around. He was cool, always giving the boys change. I think he knew I liked him, and well, he made his move."

"Can I kill the motherfucker now?" he asked, not really wanting to hear the rest of the story. He heard enough from his aunt. He wasn't speaking to his mother at all. He told them she was dead to him even though he didn't mean it. He just wasn't fucking with her right then.

"Ish, please," she sighed, rubbing his stomach before she wrapped her arm around him. "He's already suffering." She heard he was using his own supply, and barely making ends meet.

"That makes what he did right?"

"I'm not saying that, Ishmael," she said, sitting all the way up. "But what does that change? I went from being a nobody to now the entire world knowing me and for what? An amateur sex tape? One I didn't even know really existed?"

"Fuck that tape and fuck them," he told her, pulling her towards him as he kissed her forehead. "Kim Kardashian bounced back. Hell, it actually helped her and that damn Mimi from that hip-hop show. Her no talent ass. I wish a motherfucker would speak on you," he growled, making he smile. She still didn't feel any better but him standing up for her helped just a little.

"I heard your mother had something to do with it," she said lowly. She didn't hate his mother, but she wasn't too excited about meeting her now.

"Later for that. So, Mercedes," he said, kissing her forehead once more. "I can't do Myriah right now. A'ight."

"Yeah, I guess," she said, understanding. She couldn't do Carrie either, so they were in the same headspace when it came to mothers.

"Old news and probably not my baby. Timeline isn't off since I fucked her six months ago, but who knows how far along she is. The bitch is a liar," he fumed. "But if it is..."

"I know, Ishmael. I know," she said, finishing up for him.

"I have to. I'm not built like that. I have to be there for my kid. Not her, but definitely my kid."

"As you should. It's exactly why I uh, I love you," she said quickly, shutting her mouth fast.

"You what?" he asked, smiling. She never said it. Well, not first or like she was in love with him.

"Ugh, I love you," she giggled. "I'm in love with you."

"With me? Ishmael 'The Fuck Up' Payne?"

"Ishmael 'The One I Can't Live Without' Payne. And don't you ever call yourself a fuck up, ever. It's me that's the fuck up."

"Yo, Pep. Naw, ma. Never that."

"So, we back to ma again?" she asked him, shooting him a look through squinted eyes.

"Hell yeah," he laughed, waving Drew and Blake over that stood with Sashay and Fat Fat.

"Now move with your cry baby ass. Let me go holler at my little niggas," he told her. "I owe them an apology."

"Ugh, I hate you," she said.

"Naw, you don't," he said and stopped, before he got up. "You could because what I did was fucked up and if you never speak to my mother, I can't say shit. It was foul on all kinds of levels, but please don't penalize me, Pep. Don't take the best thing that has ever happened to me away from me."

"The best thing? And what is that?"

"You, " he said, lightly pinching her cheek. "You, Pepper Murphy."

EPILOGUE

CHRISTMAS MORNING

" *L* et the church say amen."

"Amen," they all said.

"And amen," Pastor Kirk said, smiling at the church filled from pew to pew. "It's good to be in the house of the Lord. Today's scripture usually comes from Matthew one and eighteen, which focuses on the birth of Christ, but I want to focus on another one. Mark fourteen, when Judas betrayed the Christ."

Pastor Kirk had been pastoring for a while, watching many in his church raise their children. When Skebo and his wife joined earlier this year looking to become more active, they brought the others with them. After the scandal went viral, the Pastor reached out to him. He told them to come to the house of the Lord where forgiveness could take place.

At first Chico declined, not even speaking to his wife, but with urging from the others, he got his family up and came.

"Jesus was loved by many but hated my more. Hated so much the the ones you love, have an assignment given to them to show you that betrayal comes but blessings come right behind them."

"Take you time, Pastor!" Mother Washington yelled out, causing them all to laugh.

Pepper snickered, shooting her eyes at Ishmael who's face was sullen. While he refused to go back home, staying cooped up in the hotel with them, his heart was hurting. He still hadn't spoken to his mother who was sitting just a few pews behind them. She thought all the mothers were funny, even the praise dancers who were scowls on their faces as they danced passionately, hoping to get a smile out of him, but she couldn't.

"I'm trying Mother Washington but I hear First Lady Kirk has Christmas dinner all ready to go, so I'll have to put some gas on this one," he said, causing everyone to laugh even more.

By the time he was done, the spirit was high. People were in the isles crying, waving their hands in the air as they cried out to God asking for forgiveness. Ishmael was full, crying himself as Pepper rubbed his back. He was tired of hurting, wondering when his mother would decided when enough was enough.

Myriah could barely breathe, holding her stomach as she cried out to God herself. Chico came home, but refused to sleep in the same room with her. She was now at her lowest point. The only other time is when she tried to kill herself the night Keyz discovered Ishmael wasn't his.

She wanted God to take this pain away, her voice piercing the air The louder she wailed, the more Ishmael cried. He wanted to run to hear, but was confused. He rocked back and forth as Pepper told him it would be okay.

"I need to see her," he whispered, looking her way. His face was wet and his eyes were red. "Baby, I need to see her and ask her why."

"You sure?" she asked him. He nodded his head yes.

"Okay, baby. Come on, let's go." She slipped her hand in his and stood as he followed suit. The walk felt long and heavy but he felt lighter the closer he got to his mother. He never once wanted to hate someone so bad but couldn't. As he reached down to get her attention, she reached up and grabbed his hand. He didn't know if she knew who's hand it was but she stood, pulling him to her when she did.

"I'm so sorry, Ishmael. Oh God, please let him forgive God. I'm done. I swear I'm done, God. Please don't take them from me. I'm sorry, so sorry," she cried out, grabbing Pepper's hand next. She touched her face and smiled. Then asked, "Will you forgive me...please."

Pepper wasn't sure what to do, but when she closed her eyes and took a deep breath, she heard God say *"Let it go."*

When she said "yes", the atmosphere shifted. Chico joined them, leading all four of them to the altar. By the time they made it there, Iyana and Keyz were right there with them. That day not only did they all learn about forgiveness, but Myriah asked to be baptized again.

🍃

"So, is it his?" Petey asked, sitting in the driveway for hours after looking all over for her.

"No, it's yours," she said, walking by quickly. She hated herself, but more importantly, she hated her life.

"Hey, hey, baby. Stop," he said, grabbing her hand before she went in. "That's a good thing, right?"

"I don't know," she sniffled. "Is it?"

"Shit, well it better be because after today, I work for me," he said, pulling his cell. He logged into his bank account, one he had never touched short of depositing money. It contained one point five million dollars.

"Oh my, baby. What's this?"

"It's ours, Mercedes. I know I'm stupid, really stupid. I've made some mistakes," he said, slowly lowering to one knee.

"Wait, wait," she said nervously, covering her mouth. "I just—"

"I know what you did and why, but I'm partly to blame. Let me make it right and no, I'm not asking because of the baby," he said, lightly touching her stomach. "I'm asking because I'm tired of chasing shit when what and who I want is right here."

"Are you sure?" she asked, wondering what Paris was going to think.

"I think you should say yes, baby," they both heard Big Wayne say with a mad Paris by his side. She couldn't believe Myriah had tricked her baby girl into getting involved with such a scandal, but the morning blogs set the record straight.

Myriah admitted to her wrong doing, even apologizing to Mercedes. She even went as far to tell Petey to grab on to her and love her now before she ended up like her.

"Sir?" Petey said, about to stand up.

"Naw, stay down there. My baby girl ain't answered you yet," he said and laughed, nudging Paris.

"Oh, shut up," she grumbled, then broke out in a laugh herself. She was miserable. Totally miserable, but she saw something on her daughter's face she had never seen before—total happiness.

NEW YEAR'S EVE

"Authorities have arrested Bernard Johnson along with accomplice, Carrie Murphy, for not on a sex trafficking but drug trafficking. too. Videos that surfaced not only showed Carrie's daughter partaking in sexual acts while under the influence of drugs, but..."

It was New Year's Eve and they all were at the Ramos household sitting around to bring in the New Year. Christmas morning turned out to be something no one had ever expected. Myriah not only offered a formal apology, contacting The Shade Room, TMZ and !EOnline, but she worked with authorities, even telling the role she played in getting the sex tapes leak in exchange for not being prosecuted.

Admittedly, she didn't know how old Pepper was at the time, but she finally came to grips with herself that hurt people really do hurt people. The Monday after Sunday service, she and Chico went and signed up for counseling to repair their marriage once again and her for individual counseling.

As a part of her offer to remain free, Myriah went on to make a very large contribution to the Camillus and Phoenix House, two programs that took in victims of homelessness, substance abuse, mental health, and sex trafficking.

As they all looked at the news, Pepper sat there with mixed emotions. She loved her mother, but to know she was a part of something so hideous made her question parenthood altogether.

"Hey, want to talk?" Iyana asked her, coming over and taking a seat next to her. The men were all out back, firing up the grill with the kids, including Drew and Blake, while the women were in the house handling the sides.

"No, not really," she said, quietly as took a deep breath. "I'm sorry."

"Please, don't apologize, ever. I just wanted you to know you're not in this alone. You have a new family now."

"Do I?" she asked, still wondering what would happen next. Department of Children and Families had already contacted her to interview the children who were both deemed to have no available, legal caregiver. She was more worried about than herself.

"You sure do," she said. "Chase has already filed the necessary paperwork. There is no way they can use anything against you when you were a child."

Chase was Iyana's sister-in-law, was a kick ass attorney. Family law wasn't her specialty, but family was. Without hesitation, she flew right up to North Carolina, petitioning the courts on Pepper's behalf.

"And what about Mercedes? She's family, too."

"The baby isn't his we heard, but even if it were, nothing changes, Pepper. You are a still Payne."

"I am? Funny seeing as if my last name is Murphy, but okay. You're too kind, Miss Iyana."

"No, it's just Iyana. Well, Auntie Iyana or mom," she said with a warm smile, grabbing her hand.

"I don't know, but thank you," Pepper said, still feeling overwhelmed.

When they both looked up, there stood Ishmael looking all delicious, a grown ass man with his bearing neatly shaved. He smelled like a million bucks, his scented cologne mesmerizing her. His hair neatly braided down by her hands, he could still feel it, wishing he was in between her legs right now.

Wearing a cream, red and gold Nike sweat suit, he winked at her as she checked him out. He'd bought the same one for Pepper and the boys, making them take Christmas pictures early that day outside. They planned to take Christmas pictures after the holidays, but he just couldn't' wait.

"I think I'm in the way," she whispered, standing up as she took her husband's hand.

"Miss Iyana. Wait, I—"

"Woman, hush that fuss. And you don't' listen. It's auntie or mama," Ish told her, then dropped on not one, but down two knees.

"I uh. I think, I think…"

"I think she acting slow. You slow, too?" Blooney asked Sashay who popped him when he did.

"Boy, shut up. Dang," she grumbled, being careful not to curse in front of Fat Fat. Blooney wasn't trying to be daddy, but he was nipping all that cursing in the bud when Fat Fat covered his mouth like "ohhh".

"She didn't curse, Fat Fat," Blooney said, taking him from Sashay. "She know better."

"Yessss," Chizon said, making everyone laughed. "Her know better."

"Get your son, Chico," Myriah said quietly, just grateful she could be there to witness her son truly step up and be a man. She fell back right after she did, still slightly embarrassed.

"Well, nephew, let's do it," Chello told him, ready to eat. "I got a party to plan tonight, so hurry it up." Mulan grinned, holding on to his waist. He was about to make his announcement, a dream finally coming true after all this time.

"Pepper Murphy, since the day I met you, I was a pain in your ass."

"Ass!" Fat Fat said.

"Damn it," Blooney said and sighed, popping Ish. "Language, bro. Language." Kevin snickered, glad he hadn't caught the love bug yet. He was eyeing all the single women in the room, ready to go in for the kill.

"Bruh," he said until Keyz cleared his throat, motioning for him to focus. "Sorry, dad. Like I said, I was a pain in the butt. I was bossy, forcing my way into your life. I ate all your food, and made you do my homework. Oh, and that paper you wrote for English 101 was lit, baby girl. I swear you're the sh—it, ma." Everyone laughed.

"This is *your* son babbling," Keyz told Chico. "I'm smooth with mine," he said, winking at his wife.

"Whatever," Iyana said, then kissed his on his neck slow and soft. "You are smooth," she giggled, so smooth she said, then placed his hand on her stomach. He gave her a look like he was confused, then his eyes grew.

"Naw, no way."

"Yes, way. Now you hush and listen."

He was now the babbling fool, trying to tell everyone what he just learned, while Iyana covered his mouth. She knew that would get him, glad he couldn't contain himself. This would be baby number four and she was done.

"Anyway," Ishmael said loudly, pulling out her ring. It was a 2.5 rose gold single diamond, perfect against her chocolate skin. "Pepper Renesha Murphy, would you do me the honor of being my wife?"

"Yesssss!" Chizon shouted, making them all laugh again. Especially Fat Fat who clapped his hands.

"Dat's Peppa," he whispered to Blooney, blushing.

"Bruh, I think shorty has a crush on your girl," Blooney said, tickling Fat Fat.

"This has got to be the longest proposal a nigga *never* heard," Kevin groaned, shaking his head when Pepper finally shouted, "Yes, yes! Of course I will!" She bent down too, taking a deep breath as she kissed him good and long. He hummed lowly in her mouth as they room broke out in a cheer.

Drew and Blake ran towards them, knocking Ishmael down right before he slipped the ring on her finger. He couldn't remember in all of his years, even on the court, he had ever been so happy.

"She said yes, my niggas!" Ishmael yelled out, while they all clapped. "I love you Pepper," he whispered, pulling her down to him.

"Not as much as I love you. Thank you, Ishmael. Thank you for choosing me."

"No, baby. You chose me. You had a choice. Remember, you always do," he told, confirming her worth. He was going to break her out of that, but for now, he just wanted to relish in her presence as his entire family looked on.

When everyone started to pack up, taking plates to go before the clock struck twelve, Myriah walked up slowly to the couple, taking a deep breath. They'd sat out by the pool, watching the stars and fireworks that shot up in the air.

"So, I said yes," she said, patting Ishmael on the leg so he would give them some privacy.

"You sure?" he asked, still not trusting his mother as far as he could see her.

"Yes, baby. I'm sure." Getting up, he kissed on the forehead, then hugged his mother quickly before he took off.

"Yes you did and I'm glad," Myriah confessed, praying her future daughter-in-law knew she meant it. She smiled, this time it seemed genuine. "You know, Pepper, everything I did, was done because I love him. Not because I hate you."

"I know," Pepper added quickly, not wanting to have this conversation. They weren't cool like that and it was too soon to speak so frankly. She had to forgive, but Myriah was no different than her mother. She younger, drug free and covered hers up very well. Yet, for the sake of Ishmael, she was willing to try.

"And I was wrong. I'm getting the help I need, Pepper. Please don't let what me or your mother did ever make you feel you don't deserve the best. So, as a gift from me to you, here you go," she said, handing her a check for two hundred thousands dollars. "For school or whatever you want to do with it. An early wedding gift."

"No, no," she said, covering her mouth as she looked at it. "I can't take this."

"Yes, you will. We insist," Chico said, grabbing his wife's hand.

"And this," Keyz said, handing her another envelope. When she opened it, it was a deed to their own house in North Carolina.

"Wait, I uh... Oh my."

"You really do deserve it," Iyana said, pulling her in for a hug. "And thank you. Thank you for loving all of us anyway."

"But mostly for loving my ignorant ass," Ishmael said, walking up and grabbing his girl from behind. "Now, you old folks can run along and go to bed. I got a fiancé' I want to go show off. Call up The Shade Room and put that out there, ma."

"I hate you," his mother laughed, wagging her finger.

"But I love you. And thanks, ma. I really do love her.

"I know you do, baby. I know."

"Hey, it's almost midnight," Chico yelled out. "Grab a glass."

When the clock stroked twelve at midnight, they all sang and toasted to a new year. A new year of love, laughter, new blessings, but most of all, new beginnings.

The End

THANK YOU!

Happy holidays from my family and me to yours! If you have gotten this far, please do not hesitate to leave me an honest review. This is my first independent project, but God Willing, not my last.

I wasn't sure what would pour out of me when I started this, but as always, God received the glory. If you like any couple, shout them out in the review. They might pop up and speak back when I see it. Who knows. Stay tuned for my next standalone...Chasing Footsteps coming soon!

CPSIA information can be obtained
at www.ICGtesting.com
Printed in the USA
LVHW091703220120
644442LV00005B/962